A sheriff in search of a killer.
He didn't know how badly things would go wrong.

The horse suddenly dropped and rolled over on its side. Bud was too startled by the sudden attack to pull his leg free of the stirrup; then he realized it was simply too late to do anything but lie there with his right leg pinned under the weight of the saddle and the body of the horse.

He was aware enough to get his pistol free of his holster, but he couldn't see over the bulk of the horse. Michelle bolted past him, took up a shooter's stance and emptied all fifteen rounds from her 40-caliber Glock, hit the eject button, and slammed another clip home.

Bud was shouting, "Take some cover, damn it! Take some cover!" And then she was out of sight.

OTHER WORKS BY ROD COLLINS

FICTION
The Sheriff Bud Blair Oregon Mystery Series
Stone Fly
Bloodstone
Mariah's Song
Not Before Midnight

~

The John Bitter Post-Civil War Series
Bitter's Run
Abiqua

NON-FICTION
What Do I Do When I Get There?:
A New Manager's Guidebook

SPIDER SILK

Rod Collins

BRIGHTWORKSPRESS

SPIDER SILK
[REVISED EDITION]

Bright Works Press
Redmond, OR 97756
brightworkspress.com

First Edition, © 2008, Rodney D. Collins
Revised Edition, © 2022, Rodney D. Collins

All rights reserved
All rights reserved. No part of this book may be reprinted or reproduced or utilized in any form or by any electronic, mechanical, or other means, now known or hereafter invented, including photocopying and recording, or in information storage or retrieval systems, without permission in writing from the author.

This is a work of fiction.
Names, characters, places, and incidents are the product of the author's imagination and are used fictitiously. Any resemblance to actual persons, living or dead, or events is entirely coincidental.

Cover Design by Val Stilwell and Anne Starke
Growth Collaborative • Eugene, Oregon
growthcollab.com

Book Design & Production by Eva Long
longonbooks.com

Print ISBN 979-8-9895768-3-8

Printed in the United States of America

to Vi

PROLOGUE

MAYBE IT WAS his version of a mid-life crisis, born of monotony, boredom, and a fleeting sense of his mortality.

But he wasn't the Harley, earring, tear-up-your-life-and-start-over type. He was cerebral. So he began to siphon small amounts of money into dummy accounts. He kept telling himself if he was caught he could argue it was simply a way to test the bank's computer security system, and then put the money back. No harm, no foul.

But when Susan McDowell, a senior teller, made an unannounced visit, it all changed. She knocked firmly on the door to his office, the one bearing a discrete brass plaque that read Truman W. Conover, Vice President for Investment Banking. She entered without waiting for an invitation and closed the door behind her. At five feet two she was almost tiny, but she had a full figure, a clear complexion, long brown hair, and cool blue eyes.

"Mr. Conover," she began, "you are a thief, but not a very good one." She walked around the desk and placed a folder of computer printouts in front of him. "Clumsy, very clumsy."

"I don't know what you are talking about," he blustered.

"Yes, you do." She pointed to two columns of numbers on the top sheet of the file. And then just looked at him.

He shook his head, ran a hand through his wavy brown hair, and then composed himself. "I don't think you understand. This was just a way to test our security system."

"Oh, Mr. Conover. You could have made that argument earlier, but when you bought the cabin cruiser, you crossed the line. You should not have used your personal line of credit to pay the balance. You see, Mr. Conover, you left $60,000 accounting tracks all over your theft."

He took a deep breath and stood towering over the small woman. He looked into her cool blue eyes and asked, "Who else knows?"

She stared up at him, silent for a minute, hearing the menace in his voice. "Let's get the rules straight. I have copies of these documents, and others equally damning, in a sealed envelope that will be delivered to the DA if I die from unnatural causes. And, no, I will not tell you the name of my attorney."

His anger washed out in despair, he flopped back into his expensive leather chair, slapped the desk with the flat of his hand, and in a low voice growled, "Shit, shit, shit!"

"You have the right idea," she continued, ignoring his outburst, "but you aren't very good at this. Now here's what we're going to do. First, you're going to put this money back. I'll help you do that. No one will ever know there was a discrepancy. Then we're going to start again, my way."

"You aren't going to report me?"

"Oh, Mr. Conover." She stared into his green eyes, ran her fingers lightly through his wavy brown hair and smiled. "Why do that when we have much more interesting things to do?"

CHAPTER 1

Henry "Bud" Blair woke with a start, the sheets soaked with sweat. The red glow of the bedside clock read 6:05 a.m. Just a booze dream. But it was the same recurring dream. The bullet always hit him dead center, right in the chest, coming in slow motion, visible. And he couldn't do anything to stop it.

He sat on the edge of the bed for a few minutes, knowing sleep was impossible. Damn. What was I thinking? First time I've had more than a drink in almost four years and I get half drunk. Again. He thought about the last episode, the Big One over four years ago. He had been drinking in a Portland bar, The Greek's, a cop bar haunted by uniformed street cops, detectives…the usual crowd of wannabes, camp followers, and groupies.

They gathered after hours to decompress, swap stories, bemoan the lack of community support, cuss the press, and get drunk. Bud's stops had become part of his evening ritual.

Dell BeBe, a burly black detective with a sour reputation for unorthodox methods, was telling him to slow down. When Bud ignored him and signaled the barmaid for another round, BB growled, "Look Honky, you turnin' into a lush. You used to be a good detective, but lately you just goin' through the motions. If you had your head on straight, we might have taken that kid in alive."

"Screw you, BB! I do my job, and you know it. At least I don't pull shitty stunts like stealing a punk's driver's license and sweating him 'til he bleeds."

The bar crowd had gotten quieter as their voices rose, the boozers easing in to hear the angry sparring between the two long-time partners.

"You stupid shit, you know that's how I work my snitches."

"Yeah, and they just love you, BB. Just love you. One of these days they're gonna set you up and bang-bang, we both get killed."

"Bullshit! You losin' your nerve cause you got shot. If you hadn't played the hero, that kid would still be alive."

The bar crowd would swear later that even the jukebox stopped—it was that quiet. They said Bud just sat there on the barstool for a long ten seconds, slid off, and smacked ol' BB with a hard left.

BB went flying off the stool and landed on his back. But BB didn't stay down. He shook his head, growled, got a knee under him, stood back up, took a step toward Bud, hit him once in the belly and once on the chin.

Bud staggered back, plopped on his butt, turned sideways gagging and puking on somebody's shiny black shoes.

The next morning brought a pounding headache. He vaguely remembered BB helping him up, then steering him through the door and into a cab.

It was 9:00 a.m. before the captain called them into his office. He didn't offer them a chair, just looked at them, staring first at the tape on BB's broken nose and then at Bud's swollen mouth. He came around from behind his desk and sat on the front edge, arms crossed.

"Okay. What I want to know is who started it."

BB and Bud had looked at each other, tried hard to control their expressions and finally started grinning as they pointed to each other and said almost in unison, "He did."

The captain grimaced. "Right. Thanks for the bullshit. BB, would you mind stepping out?"

BB turned and eased out the door, closing it softly behind him.

The captain stared at Bud for a long minute. "You know, what my guys do after hours is their business. You wanna have a drink, that's okay. But what I'm hearing is that one of my senior detectives is spending way too much time at The Greek's. Way too much because it's following him back to the job. You understand what I'm saying? Look at you. You can't work like that. Either you get on top of this business or join AA."

"Won't happen again, boss. I'll take care of it."

"You damn well better."

As Bud headed for the door, his boss said, "Hold on. You ever think about a change of scenery?" He handed Bud a job advertisement for an undersheriff in Lake County. "I just happen to be good friends with Sheriff Condon."

Bud looked at the flyer. "You firing me?"

"Nothing like that. Your reputation is still good, but the way you been acting it won't stay that way."

Bud just stared hard into the captain's eyes for a long fifteen seconds. "Why don't I take the day off."

"Good news. Now get out of here. I've got work to do."

As he closed the door, Bud thought he could hear the Captain chuckle and mutter something like "…on old Elroy's shoes, huh?" Bud read the Lakeview job flyer as he walked down the hall, his shoes almost silent on the worn gray linoleum. He paused as he passed BB's office door, then shook his head, folded the flyer and stuffed it in his back pocket.

He walked out the back door of the precinct and down the three short blocks to The Greek's, ignoring the light mist the locals called "Oregon sunshine" that silently dampened the streets.

When he walked into The Greek's, Rachael, his long-time bartender was behind the bar. She looked up, shook her head, and finished filling the dishwasher. Bud slid onto a stool and watched.

Finally, Rachael said, "Kinda early, Bud."

"I'm not on duty."

"You on administrative leave?" she asked.

"No, not that it's any of your business."

She pointed a finger at Bud and said, "It is when you start fights in my bar. There won't be a next time, Bud. If you start trouble in here again, you're out. This place will be off limits."

Red-faced, Bud said, "Point taken, Rachael. Hell, I'm sorry. I don't know what got into me."

"The hell you don't. You drink too much, much too often."

"Am I good for one more beer?"

"One is all you get," she said as she reached for a beer glass from a rack behind the counter.

Before she could pull the handle on the tap, Bud said, "Rachael, maybe I better have a cup of coffee instead."

He sipped the rancid coffee without making a face, then pulled the flyer from his hip pocket, reread it, and then laid it down on the bar top.

What a mess, he thought. Smack my best friend in the mouth, get shot, ignore my wife, and drink too damned much. And I think the Captain just told me I'm about to lose my job. Eleven years down the tube.

***

A month later BB pulled his red Corvette into Bud's driveway, looked at the stacks of packing boxes in the garage, shook his head, and then knocked on the front door.

Bud looked though the peephole and opened the door. "You lookin' better, Honky. Linda home?"

"She's gone. Long gone. She's divorcing me."

"Cause of the booze?"

"No, not really. Maybe just too much time alone, too much of my job. Hell, who knows."

"Jesus, Honky, you never let on. I must be some sorry-assed detective. Didn't have a clue. You get shot, your wife leaves you, your partner beats on your ass." BB paused, looking out the window, not really seeing any of the yard. "I hear you gonna be some candy-ass deputy sheriff out in the sticks."

In his best John Wayne impersonation, which wasn't all that good, Bud answered, "Wall, pardner, it's a tough job chasin' rustlers, but a man's gotta do what a man's gotta do."

BB grimaced. "You gotta work on that." He waited and then finally said, "I'm sure sorry about things, how they worked out."

"It's okay, BB. I need a change."

"You healin' up?"

Bud rubbed his sternum and grinned. "It only hurts when I laugh."

"Good thing you was wearin' your vest. Course he could've shot you in the head and then you wouldn't been hurt." He started chuckling. "Well you take care, my man. You been a good partner. We had some times, didn't we?"

"Yeah, BB we did." He stuck out his hand and they shook. "We still friends?"

"Hell yes, Honky."

The handshake turned into a bear hug and each tried hard to keep the tears at bay.

***

Bud shrugged off dreams of bullets and memories of his former life and headed for the shower.

He could smell fresh coffee as he walked down the stairs from the sleeping loft of his father's small riverside chalet.

His father, big shoulders slumped under a red flannel shirt, sat at the kitchen table sipping coffee and reading the morning paper. His dad just pointed to the coffeepot and went back to reading.

Bud carried his coffee out on the deck, set it on the wide rail, took a deep breath of cool morning air, and watched a pair of mallards drifting in the current of the eddy where the Little Deschutes entered the main river.

He listened to a robin high in the lodgepole thicket near the house, trilling his "cheer-up, cheerily, cheer-up" morning song, and his tension eased.

Molly, his little black Labrador retriever, barked for attention from around the side of house where she was chained to a tree by the lean-to woodshed.

"You born in a barn? It's cold in here."

Bud chuckled, went back into the breakfast nook, and closed the door behind him. "Well, that sets the mood. You always this friendly in the morning?"

His father straightened, folded the paper and put it on the table. "Only when I sit up half the night wasting good whiskey on a rascal."

Bud studied the half-empty fifth of Bushmills and two empty glasses sitting by the kitchen sink. He looked at his father and grinned. "Well, we didn't do too much damage. But I wouldn't say it was wasted. And I wouldn't say it was good whiskey either."

"Huh. Bring your own next time." The elder Blair toed an empty chair. "Here, have a sit. You know, it was good to have some conversation for a change. With your mother gone, I don't have anyone to talk to."

Bud could see the older man's eyes beginning to mist up. "What about that widow woman in La Pine?"

"It's not the same." The old man took a sip of coffee and glanced out at the river.

"So, you really like that sheriff business. It's odd how it all works out. Your old man is a gypo logger, poaches a little venison now and then, and one of his sons turns cop. The other turns into a pinko college school marm. You'd think one of them would have had enough sense to come logging with me."

"As I recall, when I wanted to go to logging, you said, 'No, get an education and then think about it.' That's what you said. And then you sold out and bought yourself a hardware store. That's what happened."

"Yeah, and you're still alive. Hell, for that matter, I'm still alive. I sure didn't want to kill one of my kids in the woods." He paused, looked at Bud. "You hear from your big brother lately? I sure as hell haven't."

"No. I think he's written us off as establishment types. Pro-logger and bigoted cop."

"How can you do that? Just write off your brother and your dad, say to yourself, 'Carl Blair and my brother Henry are the enemy?"

"Dad, I just don't know. I guess you just wake up one day and realize that's what happened. I do miss Maddy and the girls, but I don't think I'll be going to Illinois anytime soon."

"You ever miss Linda?"

"Not so much anymore. Hell, we weren't spending any time together as it was."

"Sexy woman. I always liked that husky voice. Do you think she got sucked into that woman's lib stuff?"

"Don't know. Maybe. But I know I neglected her some, too."

"How come you two never had any kids?"

"Dad, don't you ever give up?"

"Nope. You gonna get me a grandson one of these days?"

Bud's cell phone buzzed. He checked the number. "Looks like Lake County wants to talk."

***

Sonny Sixkiller was laying out yellow Crime Scene ribbon when his cell phone chimed. "Sixkiller."

Bud growled, "This had better be good."

"Good morning to you, too, Mr. Sheriff."

"Let's try that again. Good morning, Mr. Sixkiller. And what important business compels you to call me this time of morning?"

Sixkiller chuckled. "Well, that's better. Not good, just better. Boss, I called to let you know that Gordon Gooding died yesterday.

He owns the first place on the left as you go up Warner Canyon. A 911 call from a Franklin Pierce said Gooding fell out of his barn loft into the yard and died from the fall. You might remember Gooding. He drove an old beat-up blue Ford. The one with the yellow left front fender."

"Yeah. I know who you mean. I should have written him up for a DUI last year."

"Do you remember he used a cane to get around?"

"Yes, I do."

"Okay, so I think that has some bearing on what I'm seeing here. I don't want to discuss this on the phone, but I've secured the scene and I've asked Michelle to help with this investigation."

"She's pretty green. What about Roger?"

"She's gotta start sometime. And Roger is chasing a meth lab out in that Christmas Valley country."

Bud nodded silently into the phone, thinking about his first homicide investigation as a rookie detective with the Portland City Police. "Okay. You have the lead. I'll be there in about two hours. Who handled the call?"

"Lakeview City Police. I was in Plush investigating a cattle theft, so Chief Hildebrand handled the call."

"Okay. I'll see you in a couple of hours." Bud killed the call.

He turned back to the table. "Dad, I hate to cut my visit short, but I need to get back to Lakeview."

"Something going on?"

"A Lake County rancher died yesterday. Sonny didn't want to discuss details on the phone."

"What about some breakfast?"

"I'll get something on the road." He finished the coffee, set the cup in the sink. He turned and looked at the weathered face of his sixty-four-year-old father. "Dad, when are you going to come and see my cabin? I finished it three years ago."

"One of these days, Son. Just as soon as I sell the store. Probably this coming summer. By the way, when's your birthday? Slipped my mind."

"Dad, I'll be thirty-nine on the twenty-third of July."

"Okay, I'll be there for your birthday."

"I'll hold you to that." Bud held out his hand. His father rose, took it in his big, gnarled fist, and squeezed...his hazel eyes starting to water.

"Thanks for coming, Son. It's been too long." He ran his left hand his over his bald head. "Hell, I think I still had hair last time."

Bud squeezed his dad's hand again. "Thanks for putting me up."

"You're welcome. And take that damned black dog with you. I like her too much."

CHAPTER 2

THE RADIO SQUAWKED and Molly sat up in the passenger seat as she recognized the voice on the radio.

"County One. This is Control."

"This is One. Go ahead."

"Morning, Sheriff. What's your location?"

"I just coffeed up at the Summer Lake Store."

"Okay. Sonny would like an ETA."

Bud looked at his watch. 8:30.

"Tell Sonny I'll be there about 9:45. I'm going to meet Roger in Paisley." He paused, thinking about Roger's yarn spinning. "Make that 10:00. Anything else on?"

"The judge asked to see you at two this afternoon. Something about budget."

"Nancy, I tell you what, call him back and tell him I'm neck deep in an investigation."

"He won't like that."

"I don't care."

The radio was silent. Finally, he amended, "Okay, tell him I'll try. But don't leave out the part about doing an investigation."

He could almost hear the smile on her face.

He eased the diesel pickup out of the parking lot of the Summer Lake Store, a combination mini-mart, gas station, post office, and social center for the few dozen people who lived along the edges of Summer Lake.

Several flights of geese, ducks, and swans lifted from the big marsh fed by the Ana River. The early spring migratory birds were arriving by the thousands.

"No bird pictures today, Molly."

The drive on Highway 31 past the Summer Lake Wildlife Refuge brought back memories of his first drive from Portland to Lakeview to interview for the job of undersheriff.

When his pickup topped the summit going through Picture Rock Pass, he had pulled over on the shoulder of the road and simply stared.

It was "right." That was the only word he could find for his first sight of the green marshes of the refuge. Like the frame on a painting, the sheer lava cliffs of Winter Rim curved in a twenty-mile arc from north to east, the dark wall of Abert Rim visible in the distance, and hills of sage rolling away to the north.

Between the tree-covered slopes below the rim and the flat pan of Summer Lake, he had seen meadow ground for haymaking or cattle grazing. And he spotted the scattered ranch houses from the telltale Lombardi poplars and the cottonwoods planted by the early pioneers. His mental vision of eastern Oregon had been desert, which it was. But this was high desert with timbered mountains, clear cold streams, and lots of lakes. It just didn't fit his stereotypical notion of cactus and sagebrush.

He spent twenty minutes that first morning fighting the early sun for a decent photograph, and he knew it wouldn't make any difference what Lake County paid their undersheriff. He wanted the job. When Sheriff Condon retired two years later, Bud ran successfully for the position of Lake County Sheriff.

Bud and three full-time deputies patrolled an 8,300 square-mile area and ministered to the law enforcement needs of some seven thousand people. The last census gave a population density of less than one person per square mile. As Bud put it, Lake County ran long on cattle, timber, and high lonesome.

CHAPTER 3

When Bud pulled into the parking lot of the Paisley Mercantile, Roger Hildebrand was leaning against the bed of the white Dodge pickup with Lake County Sheriff decals on the doors.

He was holding a paper cup of espresso and jawing with his good buddy Tom Johnson, a Forest Service law enforcement officer. He could see Johnson laughing about something.

Roger Hildebrand was Bud's deputy sheriff for the north county, and the son of Lakeview's police chief. He was a good fit for the people and the culture of the area. Burly, wide-bodied Roger was a quick-to-laugh, outgoing thirty-four-year-old, and he looked like a good ol' boy, complete with cowboy boots and a Stetson.

Except for a tour in the Marines—and a free trip to Kuwait—he'd lived most of his life in Lake County. Roger was well liked, and he was a good Irish beat cop too. There was the letter of the law, and then there was the spirit of the law. Roger made good choices about both.

In a county with sparse population, where the people knew almost everyone else, he was still considered something of a local hero from his high school days—when the Lakeview Honkers won the state football championship. Sixteen years later you could still get up a good conversation any place in the county just by asking, "Do you remember when the Honkers beat Medford?"

Bud parked beside Roger's rig and got out. "What are you two characters up to?"

Roger said, "Bud, you won't believe this." Tom started chuckling and snorting. "Joe Pennington's kids—those hell-raising red-headed twins—built a dirt ramp and tried to jump the Chewaucan River with that old green Toyota pickup Pennington drives. Just like the Dukes of Hazard."

"And...?" asked the sheriff.

"You tell him, Tom."

"Well, they tried to jump it down at the Narrows next to the bridge. It's only about thirty feet wide right there. But they didn't make it. Seems they chickened out at the last minute and hit the brakes. Their pickup floated long enough for them to climb out, and now it's stuck against the bridge abutment. Every kid in Paisley has gone down to look at it. The Pennington boys are grounded by their mama, the principal is thinking about suspending them from school, old man Pennington is talking about auto theft, and the Oregon Department of Environmental Quality is on the way."

Bud grinned and looked at Roger. "I hope you decided it wasn't within our jurisdiction."

"Well, the ramp is on the state's right-of-way and the water belongs to the state. I could have written them up for driving without a license, since they aren't quite fifteen, but I figure the boys have enough trouble headed their way to see justice done."

"Good call."

Bud opened the door to his pickup and reached in for his coffee mug. Molly's tail thumped expectantly, but he ignored her and closed the door. He leaned back against the bed of the pickup, soaking up the spring sun.

"You know, this place is growing a bit."

"Yep," Tom Johnson said. "Except for a doctor, we just about have a full-service operation here." He held up his paper cup with a Cow Patty label. "In addition to whiskey and water, you can even get a latte. If you include our new drive-through, Cow Patty's Coffee Hut, we have a grand total of seven businesses in town. Myrtle just started remodeling the motel, and you can even order a new Chevy pickup, truck, or car from the garage."

Bud looked surprised. "You can?"

"Yes sir. You can. You do know that we once had a full-fledged auto dealership here in town?"

"No, I didn't know that. What happened to it?"

"When the lumber mill closed, the owners of the dealership just quit the business. Closed the doors and fled, I guess."

"So, who runs Cow Patty's?"

"That is owned by Kim Landis. She's a yumpy. Fell in love with Paisley at the last Mosquito Festival and moved here with her German Shepherd and her Mercedes SUV. The tavern crowd doesn't think she'll last, but they like her coffee…except for that sissy latte stuff."

"Yumpy? You don't mean yuppy, do you?"

"No. Yumpy. Although in this case, she could be considered a sumpy."

Roger snorted.

"Okay, I'll bite. What's a yumpy?"

"Thank you for asking. A yumpy is a young, upwardly mobile person. Yuppy doesn't make sense, but yumpy does."

"And a sumpy?"

"That's a senior upwardly mobile person." And then Tom laughed at his own joke.

Bud looked at the town, at the big cottonwoods on the corner where the main street made a ninety-degree turn east to the irrigated hayfields beyond the town, and at the shadow cast by the big wall of Abert Rim some twenty miles off. Then he focused back on Tom and Roger. His eyes were serious and direct.

"I suppose you heard about Gooding," he said.

"Yeah. I talked to Sonny this morning," Roger replied. "I guess he thinks there's something fishy about it."

Bud was non-committal. "I guess. How're you coming on that meth lab?"

"My informant didn't show this morning. Want some help with this Gooding business?"

Bud paused for a bit, and then asked, "Roger, you've lived here all your life. What do you know about Gooding?"

CHAPTER 4

TWO RANCHERS IN wide-brimmed hats were standing on the bridge and pointing at the Pennington pickup when the sheriff's county vehicle crossed the Chewaucan at the Narrows. Bud waved, but he didn't stop. Roger's narrative had taken longer than expected. He pushed the diesel to 80 mph on the five-mile flat beyond the Narrows.

Ahead of him, the high wall of Abert Rim rose some two thousand feet above the valley floor. Running roughly north and south, Abert Rim was one of several fault rims in the county.

Some 80 miles long, it had earned worldwide fame as the longest exposed fault scarp in the U.S. Geologists came from all over the world to take photos and to just get a look at it.

In one of his politically astute moments, Colonel Fremont, an early military explorer, had named the rim and the big alkali lake at its western base "Abert" after his commanding officer.

Bud slowed for the corner where the highway turned south to cross the Chewaucan River again about two miles from Valley Falls. Here the ranchers had cleared the sagebrush, drilled wells, and installed more of the big pivot systems for irrigation. The main crop was water-hungry alfalfa.

"You know, Molly, we're still pioneering this country."

He slowed again as he neared the junction of Highways 31 and 395 and honked at Clyde Whittaker, the proprietor of the little store at Valley Falls. Clyde was pumping gas for a pickup-camper combination with California plates. He waved at the sheriff's pickup.

Bud waved back and smiled. If there was one thing Clyde liked to do, it was yarn. He was in hog heaven during the tourist season when his small RV park filled with fresh audiences for his tales.

After 80 miles of sagebrush, juniper, and alkali flats, travelers on Highway 395 heading south from Riley Junction near Burns were apt to welcome the sight of the store, the old willow trees, and the gas pumps. Like thirsty nomads finding a cool spring, they stopped.

Invariably, they would ask where the "falls" were, and that would open the door for Clyde.

"You see," he would start in, "it doesn't have anything to do with water...although we do have some of that around here. Of course, you have to be careful about drinking it, which is why I drink bottled beer. I just happen to have a supply inside. Come in and sit a spell."

In actuality, there was a small waterfall on the Chewaucan, about two miles or so north of the store. But it didn't amount to much and telling tourists about it would spoil the yarning.

When he was new to Lake County, Bud made it his business to get acquainted with the people and the country. He would be at Plush, Valley Falls, Adele, Paisley, Silver Lake, or Christmas Valley on a Saturday afternoon to sample a beer and listen to the conversations at the local watering hole.

The memory of his first stop at Valley Falls still brought a grin. Clyde asked Bud if he wanted a beer, and when Bud said, "Yes," Clyde popped the caps on two, charged Bud for both beers, and said, "Thanks."

Of course, the next time Bud stopped, Clyde set two bottles out, and when Bud asked if he was paying for both again, Clyde just grinned. "Nope. This one's on me."

Fifteen minutes south of Valley Falls, Bud turned east onto the Warner Canyon road, Highway 140 to Denio and Winnemucca, six miles north of Lakeview. He could see Gooding's house and barn a mile up the road on the left just where Warner Canyon opened up and the pine timber thinned out into the sagebrush.

The sagebrush and woofy plants had made heavy inroads on the two hundred acres of sub-irrigated pasture below the house. There were willows and a few cottonwood trees along the creek between Gooding's ranch house and the highway. An open grove of bull pine grew behind the house and barn.

He slowly crossed Gooding's old, sagging log bridge over Warner Creek. House, corrals, and barn were long past paint and repair.

As the neglected house wasted away, Gooding simply shut the doors to each room and retreated to the lean-to kitchen where he had a cot, an electric range, and a sheepherder's stove he used to heat the room.

The toilet was another lean-to addition. It had an old, galvanized shower stall, and the water heater still worked after a fashion. At night travelers on Highway 140 could see the glare of one bare light bulb through the kitchen window.

Gooding's old pickup, parked by the back door, wasn't looking a whole lot better. The tailgate refused to close, feral cracks starred the windshield, and the fenders on the right side revealed both dimples and bruises. Only the tires were new. Bud drove through the yard and out to the barn behind the house. When he pulled in beside Sonny's rig, he could see Sonny squatted on his heels studying the ground.

Sonny turned his head and said, "Hello, Boss." But he didn't rise.

Bud walked over and squatted down beside Sonny. "Finding anything?"

"Well," Sonny said, "I found this." He held up a plastic baggie with a small shard of glass about an inch long and half as wide.

It was actually two shards still joined by a torn label. "I'm not absolutely sure, but I'd bet it's a piece of a Jack Daniel's whiskey bottle. And I found this over by the old outhouse." He held up a second baggie. It held the broken neck of a whiskey bottle with the cap still screwed on.

"Do we have a crime?"

"Maybe, the scene has been tromped pretty hard by the EMTs and the Lakeview City Police." He paused, and then added almost apologetically, "But I don't think they had any reason to believe it was more than an accident, just an old man falling out of the door of his barn loft. We had a heavy rain Tuesday night, so the ground was muddy."

"But you don't think it was an accident." It was statement, question, and affirmation all rolled in one.

"Come over here and look," Sonny said as he rose, brushed the knees of his pants, and straightened to his full, lean six feet.

He led the sheriff to the open door of the barn. With the beam of his flashlight he traced a set of coming-and-going boot prints in the dust and dirt of both the barn floor and the steep, narrow set of stairs that led up to the loft.

"That's what got me to thinking. If a man climbs a set of stairs and falls out of the barn, there would only be one set of boot tracks going up the stairs.

"Or if he climbs the stairs twice and then falls there would be three sets of tracks, two going and one coming. So I'm thinking someone crossed the floor there," Sonny traced the tracks again with the beam of the flashlight, "and returned."

Bud nodded. "So, whoever made those tracks didn't fall out of the loft. Maybe someone was trying to make us think Gooding had been in the loft?"

"Right. I haven't been up to the loft yet, but I did get a clear picture of the tracks." He fished his cell phone out of his shirt pocket, turned it on and showed Bud the pictures. On the screen, there was one set of tracks going to the stairs and one set coming back.

Bud grunted assent. "What about those? Shouldn't we get a cast?" He pointed to a clear set of prints in the mud just outside the barn door, the only set of clear footprints in the whole muddy barnyard.

"I thought Michelle could take care of that when she gets here."

"Where is Michelle?"

Michelle Trivoli was a bright twenty-five-year-old graduate of Western Oregon Police Academy. Nancy Sixkiller, Sonny's older sister and the Lake County Emergency Services Dispatcher, recruited her when Bud was looking to hire a third deputy.

"I asked her to get a statement from Franklin Pierce before she comes out. He's the one who called 911. She should be here pretty soon."

"I think I'd also like to get Charlie Prince, our new state trooper, to come out."

In Bud's experience, state troopers were stationed in Lake County for one of two reasons. Either they had screwed up and were banished to Lake County, or they were bright young troopers who could cut their teeth in Lake County. Bud had a suspicion Charlie Prince was one of the bright ones.

In his prior life as a detective for the City of Portland, Bud investigated maybe twenty-five homicides. In most cases, it meant interviewing family members and friends, looking for nervous responses, looking for a motive, and learning in the process that what motivates "normal" people—greed, jealousy, hatred, love—doesn't always work when tracking criminals.

The hardest cases to solve were tied to loners. Even finding family members could pose a major problem.

Working those cases meant looking for someone who knew the victim, finding where the victim worked—or if they worked— looking for a neighborhood bar where they spent time, knocking on doors, looking for anything to give the police a lead. And sometimes it meant finally assigning them to the cold case files.

Based on what Roger related, Gooding lived alone, was mean when he was drunk (which was a lot of the time), and had buried a wife years ago. He had one son, Alfred Gooding, who joined the Navy right out of high school and hadn't been seen since.

Bud pulled his notebook from a jacket pocket and wrote "A. Lynch re mail from AG to GG."

Agness Lynch was the postmaster in Lakeview. Bud learned early on that if you want to know what is really going on in a rural area, ask the postmaster or the mail carriers. They can tell you a lot about the people they deliver to, including the names and ages of the children and the names of the dogs on their routes.

When Michelle Trivoli pulled into the barnyard, Sonny and Bud were up in the loft studying the scene and taking another series of pictures. She wheeled the white Ford Explorer around and backed in beside Bud's pickup.

Michelle was a slender, pretty young woman with long black hair, dark eyes, and regular features. She was tall. Not as tall as Bud, but nearly so at five feet ten. And Sheriff Bud thought she was bright, even if still a little green. He often said, "You can layer experience on intelligence, but you can't do it the other way around."

"Come on up," he called down to her. "And be careful not to disturb that cake of mud on the stairs."

When she reached the loft, Bud asked, "What did Pierce have to say?"

"It was really quite interesting," she began. "According to Mr. Pierce, who is the vice president of the Land and Cattleman's Bank, he was called by Mr. William Casey, whose place joins Gooding's ranch on the north. Casey asked Pierce to meet with Gooding and assure him, Gooding that is, that the Land and Cattleman's Bank was prepared to loan Mr. Casey enough money to buy the Gooding place. Pierce said the deal included a provision that Gooding could continue to live in the ranch house for the rest of his life."

"Let me guess," Sonny said. "Gooding turned Casey down."

"How did you know that?"

"Gooding is...or was...of a character to dislike bankers. I doubt he trusted anyone in Lake County."

"Well, you're right. Pierce said that was why he was acting as an intermediary. He said when he drove into the ranch yard he spotted Gooding face down in the mud below the door to the loft. He felt for a pulse and then called 911."

Sonny asked, "Did Pierce think Gooding was alive when he got here?"

"No. He said it was obvious that Gooding was dead, and it looked like he had fallen out of the hayloft. I asked why he thought that, and he said it was because of the position of the body."

"Did he use the term "the body?" the sheriff asked.

"He did."

Bud looked from Michelle to Sonny. "I find that strange. Don't you? Think about it. Pierce has known Gordon Gooding for years, probably all of Pierce's life and he doesn't say 'Gooding?' Or Mister Gooding? Or Gordon?"

Sonny nodded. "Pretty cold, I'd say."

Bud turned to Michelle. "Now look at the loft. What do you see?"

"I don't see anything, except spider webs."

"Precisely. There isn't any hay, no feed, no tack, no tools, nothing up here but dust, bird shit, and old bailing twine. So, the question is this: If Gordon Gooding fell out of his hayloft, why was he up here?"

"Well," Michelle said thoughtfully, "if Gooding did fall from this loft, the spiders have been very busy in the past few hours." She pointed to a nearly perfect web stretching across the open door.

Bud's head snapped up. "I didn't notice the web. Sonny, can you get a picture of that?"

He was quiet for a minute. "Who do we know who's an expert on spiders?"

"I'll bet County Extension would know about spiders," Sonny answered. "I also found these," he said to Michelle. He held up the broken bits of glass in their individual baggies.

"What are they?"

"I believe these are broken pieces of a whiskey bottle. It's hard to tell how long they've been in the weather," Sonny admitted, "but the label on this one is still fresh enough to suggest it hasn't been exposed to the weather very long."

"Can we get fingerprints?"

"That's the idea," Sonny answered. "If we can lift any prints from these, we can try for a match from the FBI's Automated Fingerprint Information System."

A black-and-white drove across Gooding's bridge and up to the barn where the county vehicles were parked. Trooper Charles Prince crawled out of the cruiser and straightened up. Big, even by state police standards, Trooper Prince stood six feet six inches tall and weighed a lean two hundred and forty-five pounds. It was impossible for him to wear his wide-brimmed uniform hat in the cruiser. He was just too tall.

"Morning, Charlie," Bud called down. "Come on up. And don't step on that muddy footprint on the stairs."

The planks creaked on the stairs as Prince made his way up to the loft.

Bud made the introductions. "You know Sonny, and this is our new deputy, Michelle Trivoli. This tall drink of water is Trooper Prince."

Trooper Prince asked, "Bud, how can I help?"

Bud recapped what they knew and added, "Sonny has the lead, Michelle is assisting, and I'm just the step-and-fetch-it on this one."

Sonny shook hand and said, "If you'd help Michelle search the house, it'd be much appreciated."

While Deputy Trivoli and Trooper Prince searched the old house, Sonny and Bud laid out a grid search of the barnyard and the yard of the house using yellow crime-scene ribbon.

Their search led them to a homemade walking cane about seventy-five feet from where Gooding's body was found. It was old, the handle polished by much use, made from a piece of two-inch willow limb about three feet long with a fork that served as a handle.

They measured the distance from the position of the body, or at least their best guess at the position, drove a stake in the ground, and tied a piece of flagging to the stake. They marked it "#1" on a hand-drawn sketch Bud was making of the scene. Crime scene, he thought to himself.

They placed another flagged stake where Sonny found the broken glass, and they marked it "#2." Then they stretched yellow ribbon from each stake to the estimated location of Gooding's body.

From the loft, Sonny took a series of digital shots of the flagged stakes and ribbon grid. Bud tagged the cane and glass shards.

They next searched the pickup. It was surprisingly clean inside and sported a new set of seat covers. In the glove box they found the tire warranty dated some three weeks earlier for the new tires and a letter from a land development company in Bend. An assortment of .22 caliber rounds, a matchbook, and a pair of pliers kept company with an unlabeled bottle cap in the ashtray.

Bud carefully took the letter from the envelope. It was simple and direct. A Bend development company wanted to set up an appointment to meet Mr. Gordon Gooding to discuss the possible purchase of his ranch. It was dated three weeks earlier and signed by Frederick Goff, CEO.

"Well, well," Bud said.

"What does it say, Boss?"

He handed the letter to Sonny. "What it says is we now have a motive, or a possible motive, for murder. The only question is who stood to gain from the sale of Gooding's ranch."

Sonny read the letter and gave a low whistle. "Or who stood to profit by his death."

The search of the old house turned up two half-pint fruit jars that still had a faint odor of whiskey. Michelle and Charlie bagged and labeled the fruit jars. Like his truck, the living quarters were neat and clean. He might have been an alcoholic, but Gooding was a tidy housekeeper.

When they'd done all they felt they could with the scene, Bud summed up:

"Two small shards of broken glass, attached by a label, most probably from a whiskey bottle,

"Broken neck of a glass bottle, most probably from a whiskey bottle,

"Spider webs intact across an open doorway in the end of the barn loft,

"Homemade cane found approximately 75 feet from Gooding's body,

"Letter from a development company in Bend about a possible purchase of the ranch,

"Two half-pint fruit jars, suggesting Gooding had a drink with a visitor,

"A single set of footprints leading to and from the barn loft.

Bud frowned and said, "Are we missing anything?"

"I don't think so," Sonny answered.

"In that case, let's get busy. Charlie, would you get the jars and glass to your forensic lab in Bend to see if we can get ourselves some fingerprints and maybe a DNA analysis from the saliva smears? I'd sure like to know for sure who was drinking whiskey with the old man. And I'd like them to process the cane...see what they can find."

"You bet. That's what the lab's for, and they're really good at this kind of thing. There is one catch, though." He grimaced a bit. "They charge for anything and everything they do."

Bud smiled and said, "I thought you might say that. And I have a budget meeting with Judge Lynch this afternoon. Well, do it anyway."

Trooper Prince just grinned and nodded. In law enforcement circles, Tom Lynch was famous for his parsimony.

Then Bud asked Michelle and Sonny to make a cast of the mud cake on the ladder and the footprint just outside the barn door. He held out his hand to Trooper Prince. "Charlie, thanks for the help. I need to get to town."

He looked at Sonny and Michelle. "When you two finish the cast, I want you to flag the bridge to discourage the curious. And then I want you to beat the bushes, talk to the neighbors, see if anyone noticed anything out of the ordinary.

"Sonny, you might talk to the Casey's. And Michelle, I'd like you to interview Agness Lynch, our postmistress. See if she or Gooding's mail carrier noticed anything unusual. Especially find out if his son Albert has been in touch lately. And then pull his phone records."

"Ah, well, Gooding doesn't have a phone," Michelle reported.

Sonny was silent for a minute, then said quietly to Bud, "Let's talk."

They walked around the corner of the barn, and Sonny said, "I thought I had the lead."

"Damn. I apologize. I'll get it straightened out."

"You just can't help yourself, Bud. You're just like an old war horse. When the bugles sound…"

"I know."

"Why don't you go ahead and take the lead on this case, and let me focus on the cattle rustling in Warner Valley."

"You sure?" Bud asked.

Sonny punched him lightly on the shoulder, laughed and said, "Go get 'em, Boss."

Given his budget meeting with the judge and a possible homicide investigation to pursue, Bud decided it could be a long day, so he stopped by his house on the highway north of Lakeview and put Molly in the back yard.

The geyser at Hunter's Hot Springs was spouting as he drove towards town. I need to get a picture of that one of these days, he thought for the umpteenth time. Little did he know the geyser would eventually stop altogether and his chance at a photo would be gone.

A loaded log truck ahead of him made a right to turn down the street leading to the sawmill.

Bud thought of Lakeview as the oasis of the high desert. He liked the shaded tree-lined streets and was amused by the close race between the number of churches and the number of bars. Several decent motels catered to travelers headed to or returning from Reno. Modern services reflected a community and cultural energy that belied the fact that only 2,800 people or so lived within the city limits. He hadn't yet taken the time to play the local golf course, but he intended to…one of these days…maybe. He liked the setting, the little town tucked in against the lower west slopes of the Warner Mountains, the land sloping gently south to the upper marshes of Goose Lake, a sizable body of water more than twenty miles long that shrank in the dry seasons and expanded to flood fields and drown fences in the wet years.

And he was still slightly amazed by, and always entertained by, the multitude of wild waterfowl that filled the desert flyway with great squadrons of birds in the migrating season; ducks, Canadian geese, snow geese, great white swans, and the plethora of smaller marsh birds like willets, Western avocets, snowy egrets, herons, and arctic terns.

His watch read 11:15 when he parked at the rear of the County Courthouse, a modern two-story building on a city block shaded by hundred-year-old ornamental trees Bud couldn't identify.

Technical Deputy Karen Highsmith, a buxom, five-foot-four-inch brunette who ran the jail and acted as administrative assistant for Bud, looked up from behind the booking counter.

"Good afternoon, Sheriff."

He grinned. "Now, Karen, I've been about the county's business. And I haven't had a cup of coffee in about three hours. Any new guests?"

"The city arrested a Mr. Terrance Walker for indecent exposure in the Pastime last night."

Terrance was a frequent guest at the jail. He'd methodically worked his way through the justice system, losing his driver's license permanently, his wife sporadically, his job at the mill, and most of his friends. He was friendly when sober, but out of control when drunk.

Karen started snickering and then broke into uncontrolled laughter, tears running down her cheeks.

"What's so funny?"

She finally got herself under control. "He was putting the hit on a woman at the Pastime last night. I guess he was pretty drunk and pretty loud about it. She finally said he couldn't get it up anyway and called him "Peanut Balls." So, he just dropped his trousers and asked her if those looked like peanut balls to her. And then he went from table to table asking people what they thought. Carter Jones, the bartender, called the city and two officers arrested him."

"Good Lord," Bud said.

She wiped her eyes with a Kleenex. "And Harney County is sending us two paying guests, gentlemen convicted of possession and sale of a controlled substance. That brings us to six guests."

"Business is picking up since we started renting jail space. Let's not take any more. I have a feeling we're going to need those last two beds."

When she first applied for work at the jail, Karen was a thirty-four-year-old divorcee with three teenagers to raise. Over a seven-year period, she became Bud's unofficial confidential secretary and his official deputy-in-charge. Bud relied on her to manage the jail and watch the books. It cost the county good money to keep the jail going, but with Karen's suggestion to rent jail space to other jurisdictions, the jail came closer to breaking even. Just about everyone in town except Bud knew she had a crush on the sheriff.

She handed him a call message. "A Ms. Linda Blair called. Said it was urgent that she talk to you."

"I'll be damned. Huh." He took the note and closed his office door behind him. Karen could hear a muffled conversation, and she was tempted to listen in on the extension. But she thought better of it and went back to work.

When he came back out, Bud had a slightly bemused expression on his face.

"And there's this," she said, handing Bud a folded piece of paper.

The note was from Asa Connor, editor of the Lake County News, a twice-weekly newspaper and advertiser. It read, "See me. As soon as."

For over thirty-five years, Asa Connor had been feeding news to the scattered population of Lake County. Bud thought Asa kept a nice balance between local news and items about things directly affecting the economic lives of Lake County residents, especially actions of the state legislature in Salem. In fact, Asa had better coverage of the state house than The Oregonian, the state's major newspaper.

Note in hand, Bud turned and walked down the cracked sidewalk and crossed F Street to the Lake County News building, a new, single story, red brick building that occupied a quarter-block area on the southeast corner of F and Bullard Streets.

Inside, it was clean and brightly lit. A two-sided rack displayed business supplies—the typical stuff: day-planners, note pads, pens and pencils, calendars, magic markers, staplers. Bookcases ran the length of two walls with new book issues Asa carefully chose to match the tastes of Lake County readers.

Bud suspected Asa also chose books that might gently shape the thinking in the county. Copies of the Wall Street Journal, The Oregonian, and the San Francisco Chronicle were faithfully displayed in a typical wire newspaper rack near the counter.

The bookshelves held reprints of Louis Lamour, a selection of novels by other western writers, as well as books by Tom Clancy, Dale Brown, Jack Higgins, Danielle Steele, W.E.B. Griffin, Mary Higgins Clark—the popular stuff. But there were also books on business management, psychology, arts and crafts, architecture, poetry, drama, travel, and religion.

And if he didn't have a particular title in stock, Carol Connor, Asa's thirty-one-year-old daughter who worked the counter most days, could find it on the computer for a customer. UPS would deliver a book in five days or less, depending on whether it was shipped from New York or Portland.

Asa had come to the county some thirty-five years earlier when he purchased the Lake County News from Hardin Williamson. "Almost long enough to be accepted," he once laughingly said to Bud.

Asa was quick to point out there were more master's degrees per capita in Lake County than in the rest of the West, including L.A., San Francisco, Portland, and Seattle. And it didn't matter if a lot of those degrees were in forestry, agricultural business, or range science. These were educated people, and westerners were readers regardless of education.

Carol looked up when Bud pushed through the swinging glass door with "Lake County News" stenciled in a golden arch at eye level. Reflected sunlight lit his tanned features for a moment as the door swung open. She stared, thinking *He's not pretty, but he's my idea of a man, crooked nose and all.*

"Good morning, Sheriff," she said as she smiled at Bud. "He's in back."

"Thanks, Carol. How are you today?"

"Not as busy as you must be," she answered.

His brows furrowed a bit. "You know something I don't know?"

"All I know is that Dad's had a bee in his bonnet all morning about Gordon Gooding's death. That generally means that all is not as it appears to be. And now you're here to see him. Something's up for certain when you two get together," she finished with an almost impish smile.

She wasn't tall, maybe five-foot-five. Bud could see why Sonny Sixkiller was sweet on her. Short ash-blond hair, green eyes, a small pretty face, a full figure, and a quick, playful intelligence.

"Ah, now...you're guessing that's what Asa wants to talk about because that's the only interesting thing you've heard today. He just probably wants to talk about the Pennington boys." He let that comment dangle and walked behind the counter and down the hallway that separated the offices on the right from the press room on the left.

"What about the Pennington boys?" Bud just waved.

Asa's office door was open, and Asa was behind his desk, leaning forward, his fingers pounding a keyboard with a touch that said he'd learned the keyboard on a typewriter. He was peering at a display terminal over the top of his granny glasses, an unlit pipe clenched in his teeth.

"I gave up smoking," he said when anyone commented on the pipe, "but I didn't give up pipes."

In truth, it was a useful pacifier when he was writing. He had ruined the stems of about two dozen unlit Meerschaums in the fifteen-odd years since he quit smoking. Bud asked him one time if he didn't think maybe cheap corncob pipes would work just as well.

"Nope," Asa replied. "I smoked good pipes. So that's what I chew."

Asa looked up when Bud walked in. Bud took a stack of files off the battered wooden visitor's chair and looked around for a place to put them. A bookcase and a half dozen tall filing cabinets shared the room with Asa's desk. Each cabinet, the corners of the room, and the bookcase were piled high with old newspapers, books, notes, and old business cards. Even the window ledge on the high window behind Asa supported stacks of papers.

"Put them on the floor," Asa said. Except for the freshly painted walls in a lemon hue and the framed diploma for journalism from the University of Oregon, everything appeared chaotic. Bud knew, however, that Asa had a keen memory for what each stack contained. His office was the only untidy thing in Asa's life.

"Bud," Asa said by way of greeting.

"I got your note, Asa," Bud said, and then waited.

Asa swiveled his new executive chair to the side, stretched his long legs out in front of him, and leaned back with his hands clasped behind his head. He was long-limbed, stood six foot two, and weighed in at a skinny one fifty-five. He was going bald, so he just cropped his graying hair a little shorter and let it go.

He had a habit of stooping when he talked to people because most people just weren't that tall, and Asa liked to look people in the eyes. He was a good interviewer, and people, especially women, talked about how kind his blue eyes were.

Bud was one of those people who thought out loud, which was why he had a habit of talking to Molly. But he knew that Asa would shape his thoughts in his own mind before he started talking, and the wait was always worthwhile.

Carol brought in a cup of black coffee, handed it to Bud, and gave him a dirty look. He knew she was miffed because he hadn't said more about the Pennington boys. She also knew he liked a little cream in his coffee.

"I'll get the cream when you tell me what happened to the Pennington boys," she said.

Bud chuckled. "If I didn't know any better, I'd think you were in the newspaper business." He threw up his hand, "Okay, if you get me some cream, I'll tell you before I leave."

"Deal," Carol said and left.

Asa started in. "I've been giving some thought to Gordon Gooding's death. I've known Goody for thirty-five years. When I first came into this country, Gooding was hard working. He kept his place up. The fields were tended. He seemed to make enough money to keep kith and kin in the necessaries.

"His wife, Martha, died in a car wreck about twenty years back. That's when he started drinking, and his place started going downhill. He still ran enough cows to pay the taxes and buy booze back then. But he just withdrew from the world.

"His son Al practically raised himself. When Al finished high school, he joined the Navy, and as far as I know, he never came back.

"Anyway, when Goody started drawing his Social Security, he rented pasture to Craig Casey, Bill Casey's father, sold what was left of his herd, and then got down to some serious drinking. Over time he sold all of his stock, his machinery, a few acres along the highway, and then just retreated from the world. I always expected him to die from malnutrition or cirrhosis of the liver or some such thing long before now.

"Which brings me to my point. Goody was in here a couple weeks back and paid me to have two hundred No Trespassing signs printed up. He paid us good money to have them printed on heavy stock, and plastic coated to stand the weather. I can't print on plastic stock, so I suggested he go to the Farmer and Ranchers Coop and see if they had any signs. He said no, he wanted me to do it.

"I took the order and farmed it out to a print shop in Klamath Falls. Goody paid me cash right on the spot and said he'd be back in a couple of weeks to get the signs. And I noticed something else. His old pickup had new tires. The expensive Wild Country tires Les Schwab sells.

"So, here's where my thinking takes me…or maybe it doesn't take me anyplace but to some questions. Why, after all these years, would Goody suddenly want to post his property? He didn't have an animal on the place, not even a dog. He didn't really have anything left for anyone to steal. And why this sudden interest in new tires after running on bald tires for years and years? That's good drinking money."

Bud waited for Asa to continue, but Asa just stopped talking. Bud sipped his coffee, which was still black.

Finally, Bud said, "Well, Asa, that's very peculiar. I don't have much to go on either, but I'm thinking there was more to Gooding's death than an accidental fall. Right now I just don't have a lot to go on. I did find a letter from a land development company in Bend that wants to meet Gooding to discuss buying his ranch. But that doesn't tell me who would profit from his death. You can't buy land from a dead man."

Asa scratched the bridge of his nose with a pencil eraser. "Well, you can buy it from his heirs though."

"Do you know something I should hear about? Until we get the autopsy report I don't know why, who, or how. I'm long on when, but little else."

Asa nodded, then said, "Well, it's just a rumor that Agness picked up from one of her cronies. The rumor says the Paiute Indians from Burns are looking at the land as a possible dude ranch and off-reservation casino. I'm casting my net, and so far, it's empty, but it fits with the letter."

Bud and Asa had partnered on one drug case three years earlier, one of those cases where an informant doesn't want the cops to know who he is, so he gives the paper information believing the paper won't share the source. Then the paper gives the information to the police, who then verify the validity of the information. The informant stays safely in the background.

Bud had learned to trust Asa's judgment about what to share in the paper and what to sit on. Asa was still a newspaperman, but he wasn't on a crusade to make the police look bad.

"If you add the peculiarities you told me about to what I have," Bud added, "it begins to smell a little. Off the record, I'm treating it as a homicide. I'll know more after the autopsy."

CHAPTER 5

Deputy Michelle Trivoli **parked the county's Ford Explorer** in the parking lot behind the old two-story post office. It was typical of its era, complete with marble floors and brass-fronted mailboxes. At the service counter, she asked for Agness Lynch and was shown to a small office with high windows and a beautiful old roll-top desk.

Agness, a plump sixty-year-old with neatly curled, short gray hair, waved Michelle to a chair while she finished a phone call with one of her old cronies. "My spies," she affectionately called them. Even though her position as a quasi-federal employee kept her from holding public office, Agness and her friends were a formidable political power in the county.

Agness hung up and turned to Michelle. Reading Michelle's name tag, she rose to her full five-feet-four inches and held out her hand. "Miz Trivoli, we haven't had a chance to meet. I'm Agness Lynch."

Michelle smiled and shook hands with Agness. "Please call me Michelle. It's really nice to meet you."

"What can I do for you?"

"Thank you for seeing me. I'm hoping you can tell me whether Gordon Gooding has been getting any mail from his son Alfred. Sheriff Blair said if anyone would know, it was you."

"Sit. Such a sad business." Agness plumped back in her chair. "I'm not always here, so it's possible that I missed it. But I don't think so. At least nothing recently. Except for his monthly light bill and his Social Security check, about all he ever got were local advertisers. I do remember Connie, our mail carrier, telling me about two years ago that he delivered a letter to Goody from Alfred. He commented on it because personal letters to Goody were a rarity. The postmark was someplace in Nevada, but I don't remember exactly where."

"Could you ask him if he remembers?" Michelle asked.

"I can do better than that." Agness opened a drawer and took out a cell phone. "Let's see if Connie is through the Deep Creek canyon yet. His cell phone won't work in there."

Agness dialed, hit the send button, and waited. The ringing stopped.

"Con, this is Agness. Can you hear me all right? Good. Listen, do you remember the letter Gordon Gooding got from his son Alfred? Okay. When was that? That long ago? Here's the sixty-four-dollar question. Do you remember the postmark? Okay. Thank you. A nice deputy sheriff is wanting to know."

Agness put the phone away. "Connie said Gooding got a letter from Alfred over three years ago, postmarked from Elko, Nevada. I don't want you thinking we're always so nosey, but this was so unusual that it stuck in Connie's mind."

Michelle rose to go. "Thank you, Mrs. Lynch. You've been a great help."

"Anytime, and call me Agness, please."

***

District Attorney Howard Finch, a short, portly man with a mop of curly blond hair, met Bud and Dr. John Loeffler at the Norwin Funeral Home. George Peel, mortician and lay preacher for the Community of God Church, escorted them to the embalming room that served as a temporary morgue for the county.

The mortal remains of Gordon Gooding—still in muddy jeans, a torn flannel shirt, and old cowboy boots—lay on a stainless-steel table.

"Morning, Doc," Bud said to Dr. Loeffler, a lean, gray-haired, sixty-nine-year-old retired physician who always ran unopposed as the County's Coroner. Asa once said Doc Loeffler had delivered half the babies in the county and was godfather to most of those.

"Thank you, George," Bud said by way of dismissal. George Peel hid his disappointment and quietly slipped out, closing the door behind him.

Bud turned to Finch. "I wanted to see the body before we ship Gooding to the state medical examiner. And I wanted you as a witness. I also want you to subpoena Gordon Gooding's financial records when we get through here."

Finch looked at him with a question in his blue eyes. "So, there's more here than an accident?"

"I won't know until after the State pathologist finishes his work. But it smells to high heaven. That old man didn't climb into the loft, and he didn't fall out of his barn. I can prove that much. We have enough physical evidence to suggest a fight took place, but with whom and about what I'm not sure." He looked at Doc. "Do we have an estimated time of death?"

"I met the ambulance at the hospital. Based on his body temperature at that time, I'd say he died between two and four p.m. I pronounced him DOA."

In a deep baritone voice that more than made up for his portly stature in the courtroom, Howard said, "Well, let's have the Doc here get into his County Coroner routine."

Doc nodded. "Yes. Let's see what this man can still tell us," and pulled on a pair of latex gloves.

***

Sonny Sixkiller rang the doorbell of the William Casey ranch house. It was a white, single-story rambler that would fit in any suburban neighborhood, complete with an Irish yew on each side of the front door and an attached two-car garage. The cottonwoods along the south edge of the yard were beginning to bud out.

An older, light blue Chevy Malibu was parked alongside the garage in the lane leading to the barn and equipment sheds in back. At least the car looked blue to Sonny, who had a slight problem telling blue from green.

There was a furtive stirring of the curtain on the big picture window, and a woman's silhouette. Sonny waited. He rang the bell again, and then rapped the door with a knuckle. "Mrs. Casey, are you home?"

He tried the door. It was locked. He rapped again. "Mrs. Casey, it's Sonny Sixkiller with the Sheriff's Department. Please open the door."

Melissa Casey opened the door a crack, slid the security chain free, and then backed away as she broke into tears.

"Is Bill home?" Sonny asked loudly as he unsnapped the strap on his pistol holster.

"No, he's gone."

Her face was a mass of bruises, cut lips, and a broken nose. She was holding a damp cloth to her mouth and trying hard to control her tears.

"Sit down, Mrs. Casey," he said as he took her elbow and directed her to a leather recliner. "Stay right here."

Sixkiller drew his pistol and searched the house, calling, "Mr. Casey? Are you here?"

"I told you, he's gone," Melissa said when Sixkiller came back into the living room. She cried out and held her ribs when she tried to get up from the chair.

"Please don't try to move."

He unclipped his cell phone and dialed 911. He recognized the voice on the line. "Jack, this is Deputy Sixkiller. I'm at the William Casey residence. I need an ambulance out here ASAP. I don't have an address, but it's the second place on the right after the Warner

Canyon junction, about six and a half miles north of town. It's a white house facing west. They'll see my county vehicle from the road. Tell them to get on it."

He turned to Melissa. "They'll be here in a few minutes. Can you tell me what happened?"

Melissa's eyes widened in fright and then closed as tears ran down her cheeks. She didn't answer, just shook her head.

"Where's Mr. Casey?"

Again, she just shook her head.

"Mrs. Casey, do you have any children?" he asked after spotting framed pictures on the wall above the fireplace. There were several photos of a young man and a young woman holding a baby, then one of a toddler, then a preschooler—the picture history of a normal, loving family.

She whispered, "Lucinda. She's in school. Seventh grade."

"Pretty girl," Sonny observed. "You must be proud of her."

Another nod.

"Did Bill do this to you?" he asked.

She just shook her head, a look of panic in her eyes. "Did someone else do this?"

Again, she just shook her head.

"It's okay, Mrs. Casey. We'll talk later. May I search the house?"

This time she nodded assent. The bedroom was total chaos, lamps knocked over, blood stains on the comforter, broken cosmetic bottles in the sink of the master bath, clothes strewn about, some still on hangers, the window blind hanging at a crazy angle from one corner.

It looked like someone just went berserk.

The rest of the house looked pretty normal, but there was a glass sitting on the kitchen counter that smelled of whiskey, and there was an empty quart of Jack Daniel's in the trash under the sink. He found a plastic grocery bag and bagged the bottle.

When Sonny returned to the living room, he said, "Mrs. Casey. I know you're scared, but I need to know something. It is very important. So please help me. Okay?"

She nodded.

"Does your husband own any guns?"

Melissa looked stricken, nodded, and then started shaking and crying. "Please don't hurt him," she whimpered.

Sonny stepped outside and called the sheriff.

Bud listened quietly to Sonny's report. "Okay," he said. "I'll get Michelle down to the hospital. Mrs. Casey might find it easier to talk to another woman. And I'll get the new county mental health counselor down there too. I don't know her very well, but we'll test her metal on this one."

"How about an APB on Casey?" Sonny asked. "For assault. Boss, I think Casey is armed and should be considered dangerous. I found an insurance bill on their kitchen table for a 1998 Ford 4x4 pickup. I suspect he's driving that. And I have a photo of Casey I'm borrowing from the residence."

"When did he beat her?"

"I don't know for sure, but it was probably after the school bus picked up their daughter to take her to school. Mrs. Casey said her daughter was in school, and I can't imagine the daughter calmly heading to class after watching her dad beat her mother nearly to death. So make that sometime between nine and eleven. Mrs. Casey is frightened, but you know what she said to me?"

"No, but I can guess. She doesn't want us to hurt her husband. Right?"

"How did you know that?"

"In a prior life, I worked a few domestic abuse cases. The victims are nearly always women. And they almost always ask that we not hurt the husband. You'd have to talk to a psychologist to understand it, and I don't think they know for sure. I for damned sure don't."

There was silence for a few seconds. Bud finally said, "Well, get back in here with Casey's photo. I'll meet you at Emergency Services."

***

Nancy Sixkiller's dispatch office was in a windowless room at the rear of the Emergency Services building, which housed the fire department and ambulance services as well as emergency dispatch.

Her world was a large desk that contained three consoles, one each for the state police, the city police, and the county sheriff. It was a state-of-the-art system that could be programmed to monitor and broadcast on the frequencies used by the Forest Service, the Bureau of Land Management, the Oregon Department of Forestry, and the Oregon State Police. It was also connected via the internet to all similar emergency dispatch centers in the U.S., including Alaska, Puerto Rico, Hawaii, and Guam. It was more than a message center. For the local police, it was their eyes on the world.

When her brother and the sheriff walked through the door, Nancy Sixkiller didn't get up. Dispatchers do all their business from their ergonomically engineered chairs.

It's the same game for every dispatcher everywhere in the world. It looks easy. Just talk on the radio, keep a radio log of who called, when they called and what the dispatcher did about it. The dispatcher also needs a map of the dispatch area, location of all resources—both officers and vehicles—knowledge of local landmarks like Deep Creek, Blizzard Gap, Quartz Mountain Summit, Dog Lake, and Whiskey Springs, and unflappable confidence, because when the dispatcher says, "Go," the officer goes.

Most dispatches are routine, but on some rare occasions life-threatening situations call for steady nerves and cool judgment. If the dispatcher sends a unit to the wrong location or without adequate information, people can get hurt, or a rescue can go wrong.

Nancy Sixkiller did not make mistakes. At least, no one who knew her could remember one, unless you could call her busted marriage to a certain college professor a mistake. She never called him anything but "old what's his name."

When she split with "old what's his name," she found a job as a rookie dispatcher with the Yakima Indian Police. She felt very comfortable there, but when Sonny told her about the opening in Lakeview, she jumped at the chance.

For one thing, it was a raise in pay and a chance to see Sonny once in a while. For another it was about four hundred miles further away from her ex-spouse.

"Morning, Nancy," Bud said as he placed a handwritten description of William Casey in front of her. "The DA has issued a warrant for the arrest of William S. Casey."

She slouched back in her chair and looked at him. "Except it isn't morning. It's nearly one-thirty. Have you had any lunch?"

Bud said, "I'll admit to being hungry. It's been a busy day, and it started about six this morning.."

She glanced at Sonny. "What about you, little brother? Want to get some lunch?"

"I have other plans," he said.

"Oh, I'll bet you do," she said. "And I suppose you think Carol Connor has skipped lunch just so she can go with you."

He grinned. "I certainly hope so."

"You behave yourself, little brother."

Nancy turned to Bud. "Okay, let's get this out and then grab a bite. Right?"

"I give," Bud replied.

Nancy had queried the Oregon DMV and gotten a description of the vehicle and the license number. A city police officer named Jack Rauls knew Bill Casey and confirmed he drove a blue and white Ford 4x4. The framed photo was of a white male in his late thirties to early forties with short, brown hair.

Nancy typed out a description on her computer keyboard, clicked on a mailing list, and it was done.

Nancy picked up a phone and said, "Colonel, it's your turn." Henry Barnes wasn't a colonel. He had been a Marine sergeant in an earlier life, but in fact he was a retired Forest Service fire management officer. He worked from ten a.m. to two p.m. each day as Nancy's backup.

During his career on the Fremont National Forest, he worked large wildfires as liaison with the military. Whenever a military unit was assigned to a fire camp, Henry would ask, "What's the rank of the commanding officer?" Then he would dig into his fire pack for a small metal box that held various insignia of rank. If the commanding officer was a captain, Henry would pin captain's bars on his own lapels. He said it made it a lot easier in dealing with the captain and his subordinates.

"But the way I got to be a colonel was like this. I was on the Hatchery Complex on the Wenatchee National Forest working two big fires when we got word that a battalion of army regulars was on the way. When I asked what the rank of the commanding officer was, they told me he was a lieutenant colonel. So I got my birds out and pinned them on my collar.

"You should have seen this guy when he drove into camp. He was wearing riding boots, jodhpurs, sunglasses, and a silver helmet. He was standing up in the jeep—this being pre-Humvee days—holding on to the windshield and carrying a riding crop. You'd have thought he was George S. Patton leading an army to war, not some light colonel who was over-ranked as a battalion commander on his way to do mop-up on a fire.

"Anyway, I did my duty and welcomed this bird to camp, thanked him for coming in our hour of need, and showed him where to pitch his tents and set up his quarters. There was a nice level field with lots of room for vehicle staging and room for tents for the nine hundred men and women who were some four hours behind him. He said, 'No thanks. I'm camping down by the river.'

"I reasoned that it would not be okay. We had concerns about the impact of nine hundred people on the vegetation along the riverbank. That was why we weren't already camping in the shade ourselves.

"At which point he said, 'I'm a colonel, and I tell my people what to do and where to go.'

"At which point, I abandoned all tact and forgot my training as a liaison. I pointed to my lapels and said, 'You are a lieutenant colonel. I am a full colonel, and you will damn well camp where I tell you.'

"At which point he saluted and told his driver to take him to the field. I turned around and there was my incident commander standing at attention, holding a salute and saying, 'Any orders, Colonel, sir?'

And that's how I became a colonel in the U.S. Army---a full bull colonel."

***

When Henry came through the door, he said, "Reporting, ma'am."

"Bud and I are going to lunch. I just put out an APB on William Casey, but I think it would be a good idea to contact the La Pine, Burns, Alturas, Klamath Falls, and Winnemucca police departments to let them know Casey is someplace within about three hours of Lakeview. If I'm a bit late, can you cover for me?"

"Yes ma'am," Henry Barnes slid into the chair at the console, picked up the phone and started punching numbers.

Bud and Nancy got a booth toward the back of the Indian Village Restaurant. Nancy chose it for privacy and because she knew Bud liked to sit where he could watch the door.

"It has nothing to do with being a policeman," he once told her. "It has to do with reading too many western novels as a kid. The heroes never turned their backs to the door."

Nancy laughed at that. "Bud, you don't even carry a gun most of the time."

He grinned, the creases around his eyes becoming more pronounced. "Yeah, but I'd still like to know when to duck."

Bud ordered the eight-ounce sirloin, medium-well, fries, veggie beef soup, and coffee with cream. He never ate restaurant salad. "Too much chance of getting salmonella," he told Nancy.

Nancy just ordered hot tea.

Bud thought Nancy was just drop-dead gorgeous. She had the light shading of the Yakima's, short black hair with auburn highlights, and deep green eyes, a genetic gift from her grandfather, George O'Brien.

The navy-blue uniform of the Lakeview Police Department did nothing to hide her trim five-foot-seven-inch figure.

In the three years they had known each other, he had never spoken an affectionate word to her. He had treated her with respect and professional courtesy. But she knew he was attracted to her. And the biggest mystery to him was a belated understanding that she liked him. It showed in small ways, like today when she insisted he eat lunch. And sometimes he caught her staring at him. "I don't understand it," he would say to Molly. "I mean I can understand a man being attracted to a beautiful woman. But I don't understand what she sees in me. Hell, I'm years older than she is. Dog, sometimes I wish you could talk."

He was halfway through his second bite of steak when Nancy interrupted his carnal images of her lying in his bed.

"What?" he said. "Where did you go?"

"Uh…I didn't go anyplace."

"Yes, you did. You had that sort of focused-in-the-back-of-your-head look."

He almost groaned out loud. "Damn it, Nancy. Don't do that."

"Do what?" she asked innocently.

"You know what I mean. It's not okay to crawl around in my head."

"Why, Bud. I think you're blushing. I don't know what you were thinking, but I'd like to."

"I don't think we'd better go there." Bud said.

"Maybe we should," Nancy said. "It might be interesting."

Bud fidgeted. "Let's change the subject. So…what are you doing this weekend?"

Damn it, he thought, that's not what I meant to say.

Nancy gave him a long, intense look. He finally broke eye contact and picked up his coffee cup.

"Well," she answered in measured tones, "since I can't find anything better to do in Lakeview, I'm going to visit my mom in Ellensburg. She hasn't been feeling well lately, and I'm worried about her."

"Anything serious?" Bud was glad for the chance to talk about something else and wondered why he kept shying away from this beautiful creature.

"Not really, but she lives alone, and I don't think she eats right. Actually, I think she forgets to eat at all some days."

"That happens, I guess," he said, thinking about his own bachelor meals.

"So, what are you going to do for fun this weekend?" Nancy asked.

He looked a bit sheepish, and then said, "Well, you know about Linda, my ex-wife? Her mother died last week. I don't know why she called me. It's not like we're even friends any more. But she was pretty broken up on the phone, so I offered her the use of my cabin out at Dog Lake. She's due in here tomorrow, and then she and Molly are going to go hide out for a few days."

Nancy almost said, "You poor fool." Instead she said, "That was nice of you. And I'm sure Molly will enjoy the company."

Bud picked up the tab and paid the cashier. She was a young, high school dropout who'd gotten pregnant by a boy who fled the country when he found he was about to become a father at the ripe age of seventeen. Michelle Trivoli had tracked him down.

"So we can nail his dumb ass for child support," as she had vehemently put it.

"Hello, Sheriff. Everything all right?" the girl smiled as she made change.

"It was up to your usual standards," he said and put a five-dollar tip on the counter.

"Don't forget your appointment with Tom Lynch," Nancy said when they stepped out on the sidewalk.

"Oh, hell. I don't want to talk to Tom today. But I guess I better get over there." With a slightly troubled look in his hazel eyes, he touched Nancy's shoulder and said, "Thank you."

Nancy nodded goodbye and thought, he hasn't a clue.

***

It was three thirty when Bud walked back to his office after an hour of arguing with Tom Lynch, a local rancher duly elected as county judge and county administrator.

Elections were seven months away, and even though Tom had run unopposed in the last election, he was already on the campaign trail. He wanted the mostly conservative people of Lake County to know he ran a "tight fiscal ship." He ran the same campaign each time. And it ran very well.

When Lynch challenged the sheriff's request for an additional part-time deputy, Bud was in no mood to defend what he called a "pucker tight" budget.

He glared at the Judge and said, "It's been one hell of a day. I got up early to drive back from Sunriver, I've got a domestic violence case going, a suspicious death, and a runaway husband. I told you why I need a part-time deputy. Either cut it or approve it. I'm going back to my office. I've got work to do."

He slammed the judge's door on the way out.

***

He could see Sonny and Michelle through the front office window, obviously talking about something. But they took one look at his stormy face and stopped.

"Doesn't anybody make any damned coffee around here?" he growled, eyeballing the cold, empty coffee maker. He looked at the booking desk. "Where in the hell is Karen?"

He took a deep breath, sighed and let his shoulders sag. "You know," he said, "there are times when the best thing to do is try to do no harm. Which in this case means do nothing. I've got to call Tom back and apologize. Then I want to hear what Mrs. Casey had to say. Then Molly and I are going to the cabin for the evening. Would that be all right with you two? You can hold down the fort, and I promise to leave my cell phone on this time."

Sonny and Michelle both broke out laughing. Michelle said, "Karen's putting our two Harney County prisoners away."

"Musta been a good session with old Tom," Sonny observed and winked at Michelle.

Bud chuckled, feeling sheepish about telling Tom off.

"Oh, you know Tom. I think he's a good administrator, but he's fanatic about money. I get tired of defending our budget. When he started in about our request for a part-time deputy, it pissed me off. I told him our budget was already pucker tight, so either cut it or approve it. And then I stomped out."

Michelle and Sonny both grinned. "Good for you, Bud," Sonny said.

"I'd love to have seen that," Michelle chimed in.

"Well, I'm not proud of myself, but it felt good at the time."

"Okay," Bud said, looking in Michelle's direction without meeting her eyes. "How is Mrs. Casey?"

"Dr. Martin examined her. She has some cracked ribs, a broken nose, a big knot on her head but no concussion, two loose teeth, some cuts on the inside of her mouth that needed a couple of stitches, and bruises on her arms and thighs. It looks like her husband knocked her down and then kicked her several times."

"What did she have to say?" Sonny asked.

Michelle grew serious. "I think it was the hardest I've ever done. I just wanted to scream at her. She wouldn't tell me anything. And I kept wanting to ask why in the hell she was protecting someone who came within an inch of killing her."

"I know," Bud said. "Give her some time. Maybe the county's mental health person can get her to open up."

"Amy Woodruff's her name. She handled it better than I did. Amy said the first thing to do was get Mrs. Casey into shelter care. And then she said that once Mrs. Casey felt secure and was in a safe place, she might tell us exactly happened. Emphasis on might."

"What about her daughter?" Bud asked.

"Her name's Lucinda. Amy and the school counselor will talk to her, and then either she'll go to the shelter with her mom or find a friend to stay with tonight. Amy said the daughter wasn't the target and probably wasn't in any danger from Casey."

Bud finally met Michelle's gaze. "Okay. But do you think the daughter is in any danger?"

"Boss," she answered, "the abuser is almost always remorseful. I'd bet on Amy being right."

"Do you know that, or did you read it in a book?"

Michelle blushed and stammered. "I haven't had a lot of experience, if that's what you mean, but that's what we were taught in school."

Bud winced at his own rudeness. "Sorry. I think you're right. That squares with my experience. Well, if the daughter is staying in town, why don't you let Chief Hildebrand know what's going on. He can have a patrol car keep an eye on the residence."

"Will do."

CHAPTER 6

Bud parked the county's pickup in the driveway of his house, let Molly out of the back yard, opened the door on his personal vehicle, a late model blue club cab Dodge 4x4, and told her to get in. She was in a tail-wagging mood and went into to her typical spin on the front seat, like she was trying to make a nest in a hay field.

As a rule, Bud enjoyed the twenty-five-mile drive to Dog Lake, especially that section of the road beyond the farm fields and the pastures. The road wound west past Drews Reservoir and through the hills and the juniper and pine timber. But today he was grumpy and out of sorts. Some part of him knew it wasn't just Tom Lynch and budgets, or the beating of Melissa Casey— although domestic abuse always angered and upset him—or the anomalies of Gordon Gooding's death. That was part of the job.

He slowed for a bumpy cattle guard and then sped back up to his usual forty miles an hour on the narrow road.

He glanced at Molly with her head out the window, nose working the breeze for interesting scents, and her ears flared like wings on a plane. He laughed.

"Molly, you rascal. What're you so happy about? I have to tell you I'm hoping Linda changes her mind. I was pleased when she called, but now I'm not sure I want to see her again. At the same time, I'm curious to see her. And I really want her to see what

I built. Then I remember why I built it in the first place, and I get irritated at myself all over again."

He kept an eye out for mule deer. He'd never hit one, but he had come close a time or two. If they thought a vehicle was going to cut off their escape route, which always seemed to be on the other side of the road, sometimes the deer panicked and made heroic efforts to cross the road at the last second.

"And then I get to thinking about Nancy," he continued. "We've never even been on a real date, so why would I feel guilty about Linda coming down? Damn, you'd think by this time I would have my act together."

A small cottage had occupied the site on the shore of Dog Lake from the late 1930s until it burned down in the mid-90s. The elderly owner wasn't in a mood to face the prospect of rebuilding it, so he sold the ruins to Bud—"on the cheap," as the old man put it.

Bud built the cabin facing the lake for the view and the morning sun. Except for a couple of back windows overlooking the road, one in the loft and one on the main floor, the cabin just turned its back on the world. The metal-roofed, sage green A-frame sat on a narrow strip of land between the lake and the road. Except for weekends and summer vacation, there wasn't much traffic, so being close to the road didn't bother him too much. The plusses outweighed the minuses.

When he opened the pickup door, Molly made a dash for the dock. She had this notion the ducks might be gathered to beg some handouts from Bud. How they knew Bud was back, and then keyed in on his dock, was still a mystery.

Molly barked and Bud hollered, "Molly, you leave those ducks alone." This time of year the flotilla was mainly the mud hens—a small, black coot that always seemed to arrive before the bigger ducks started back north.

He unlocked the cabin door and then gathered an armload of kindling and stove wood from the stack near the back door. He kept the electric heat set at fifty-five degrees to keep the pipes from freezing when he was gone, but a wood fire always seemed much cozier.

When the airless Fire King was drafting nicely, he changed out of his khaki uniform and slipped into his blue jeans, tennis shoes, fleece pullover, and Blazers baseball cap. He shut the dampers on the stove and went outside to his storage shed.

A small one-car garage survived the fire. Bud's only improvement had been to paint it the same green as the cabin and put on a new metal roof. It served as storage for a fairly new fourteen-foot aluminum boat. An old refrigerator was tackle bin and worm storage.

He selected an ultralight spinning rod that was rigged for bait fishing, complete with a red and white bobber, dug a night crawler out of the worm box, and walked the path down through the willows to the small six-by-ten-foot dock.

When the bobber was on the water and the ripples had settled, he set the rod in a pole holder bolted to the dock. Bud took a deep breath and exhaled a lot of tension. He opened a covered storage box bolted to the wood planks of the dock, pulled out a folding chair, and sat down.

"Maybe the yellow perch will bite and we can have a good fish supper," he said to Molly. She ignored him and, nose to the ground, started a tail-wagging hunt past the willows and down the lakeshore.

The evening shadows were reaching across the lake. The air was chill but dead calm, and the lake was a nearly perfect mirror of the tulle fringes and the pine that grew beyond a narrow strip of meadow.

Shaped like a dog's hind leg—sort of, if you had that kind of imagination—Dog Lake was maybe four miles long, if you included the tulle marsh at the south end, and maybe a half-mile wide at the fat part.

The Mile High Bass Club worked with the Oregon Department of Fish and Wildlife to maintain a stock of largemouth, and some enterprising soul had long ago imported yellow perch. A species of brown catfish—mud cats to the locals—and a spring planting of put-and-take trout also coexisted in the lake.

Bud figured building the cabin on this little jewel of a lake kept him sane in the two years following his divorce from Linda. He hadn't consciously thought about the divorce for quite a while, but as he soaked up the quiet of the lake, he ran the old tape again.

Even after seven years, he still had a clear memory of the evening Linda told him she was moving to Vancouver, Washington, across the Columbia River from Portland. They were sitting at the kitchen table, reading the paper and watching the evening news on a small portable TV when he realized she was talking to him.

"What did you say?" he asked as her voice broke through his concentration. A pasty-faced reporter was covering a story about a gang-related killing Bud was investigating. The reporter wasn't being kind to the police department either. "…and neighbors are asking, 'What are the police doing about it?' Reporting live, this is…"

"I said I'm moving into an apartment in Vancouver. We've both been so absorbed by our jobs that we don't talk; we seldom spend time together anymore. And when we do, you are miles away thinking about the case you're working on at the moment. Tonight is just about the best example I can think of.

I'm trying to tell you I'm leaving and that I'm getting a divorce, and you aren't even listening. You're pouring over a newspaper and watching TV to see if there's anything about your latest case."

His heart was thudding as he started to get up and reach over to hug her. It was the closest to panic he'd felt in years.

"Don't," she said sharply. "You know what I'm talking about, and you'd better face up to it. You're married to your job. And I guess I'm married to mine. But whatever happened to our marriage is just that, it's not something that was nurtured. It's what just sort of 'happened.' You can't ignore a relationship and expect it to live. And I don't want to try and resuscitate it again."

He remembered the last time they had a similar conversation.

They'd spent four days boating on Hood Canal in Washington, hoping the time would help them reconnect.

"We could go to Hood Canal again," he suggested.

"No. We both just slipped right back into the old patterns, but I blame me the most. I let it happen again. Bud, we just live alone together and I don't want to do it anymore."

He finally managed to ask, "When?"

She looked sadly at his eyes where the tears were starting to spill over. "Now," she said, and pointed to a suitcase sitting in the hallway. "You never even noticed it."

***

The house sold a week after it was put on the market; they split the net proceeds and agreed on a method to divvy the household goods, the books, some old Beatles albums, and the rest. The only thing they quarreled about was the puppy, Molly. When he told Linda he was taking a job in Lake County as the undersheriff, she relented.

Molly would do better with Bud in Lake County than in an apartment in Vancouver, so Linda told him to take care of the puppy, and wished him good luck.

He felt lost during the first year. It was like there had always been a visible path into the future, and then suddenly the lights were out and he couldn't see his way anymore.

The purchase of the lot on Dog Lake had been a blessing, and although Bud had his doubts about organized religion, he thought there must have been some divine guidance at work here.

Building the A-frame had been consuming and interesting and distracting; somewhere along the way the guilt and remorse subsided, and then finally he stopped looking back and started looking to the future.

The first night he and Molly actually slept in the cabin, with a warm fire in the stove, had been simply wonderful. And walking to the dock and getting into his boat without all the hassle of backing the trailer down the boat ramp gave him an unexpected sense of luxury. When he stepped into his boat, cranked the starter and heard the motor fire up, he thought, "I'm back."

***

Molly nudged his hand with her cold wet nose, bringing him to the present.

"What do you want?"

She barked and looked at the bobber as it disappeared under the surface of the lake.

"Damn," he said. "I never really figured anything would bite in this cold water." He played a small trout and reeled it slowly in. Looking at it in the water, he said, "Nope, too small for supper." He released the trout and said, "Why don't you grow some more and then come back for another tussle."

Bud suddenly felt better than he had all day. "Come on, Molly. Let's put the pole away and open a can of stew."

***

Karen Highsmith was on the phone, and Sonny and Michelle were busy at computer terminals when Bud walked into the station at five minutes after eight, whistling a melody from the old song "Heartaches." The melody was a happy one in spite of the title.

Sonny nodded, and Michelle said, "My, aren't we happy this morning. Coffee?"

He glanced at the coffee maker in surprise. "That would be great. Thanks. Yes, I am in a good mood. Molly and I caught our first trout of the year, and I got a good night's sleep. Molly wanted to stay another day, but duty calls."

"Don't get the notion I'll do that every morning," she said pointing at the coffee maker. "This is simply a one-time aberration."

"I guess I'm not the only one in a good mood," he grinned back.

Sonny looked up over the top of the computer monitor as Bud poured a cup of coffee and stirred in some creamer.

"The state medical examiner's office called. Gooding is in their morgue. We should have an autopsy report in three or four days." Sonny reported. "And Charlie Prince sent those broken pieces of whiskey bottle to the state police forensic lab in Bend. He actually drove the hundred miles to Silver Lake and met another trooper who took them back to the lab yesterday evening."

"Wow," Bud said. "That's good service."

"And I've located Alfred Gooding," Michelle said smugly.

"How?" Bud asked.

"The internet. Yahoo People Search. You should try it sometime."

Both Sonny and Michelle had been trying to improve Bud's computer skills, and while he had a great respect for that particular tool, he still felt embarrassed and a little insecure when he strayed outside the bounds of messaging.

"Yeah, I'll do that," he replied. "So…where is he?"

"I found him in Nevada, but he moved from Elko to Ely. They pronounce it E-Lee. The Ely police will contact him and tell him about his father's death. I asked them to check their files and see if Alfred Gooding has a criminal record. He's clean in Oregon. "They'll also interview him to find out where he was in the past two days. They were very helpful. I told them we weren't sure it was an accident, but we didn't have anything concrete to go on. We were just covering the bases."

Bud nodded.

Sonny said, "We got a pretty good cast of the shoe tread on the stairs, and an excellent cast of those tracks in the doorway. Michelle and I found some old roof shakes and clamped them to the stairs just like a concrete form, and then we used that new liquid latex to fill the form. Good stuff."

"I'd like to see them."

They had a small evidence locker in a back room, just a big closet really, with a steel door and a double lock. Sonny unlocked the door and returned with casts. The date, location, and Sonny's name, rank and badge number were written on one side of each cast. He turned them bottom side up so they could examine the tread mark.

"It's not much to go on," Sonny said, "See these small, triangular protrusions? They're distinctive. Like the lugs of a walking shoe, not a hiking boot or work boot."

"That's settled then," Bud said. "Gordon Gooding didn't climb that ladder. I looked at his shoes when I was at the mortuary. The soles were as smooth as a razor strop."

"Carol Connor said he was using a homemade cane when he was in to order some No Trespassing signs," Sonny added.

"Which is another proof he didn't climb into the loft. He was crippled up, plus he had no reason to. So how did the cane wind up seventy-five feet from where his body was found?" Michelle added.

"He was fighting with someone and threw his cane at them?" Bud suggested.

"Casey," Sonny said. "Are you thinking what I'm thinking?"

"Yep. The DA better amend the warrant for Casey's arrest to include 'person of interest' in a possible homicide. Why don't you tend to that?" Bud requested.

"And Michelle, would you go talk with the EMTs who picked him up? I'd like to know if he was face down or face up when they got there. When I looked him over, he had quite a bit of mud on him, both front and back. And check with Chief Hildebrand to see if we can get a copy of their report. It's starting to come together, I think."

He turned to Karen Highsmith, who was almost hidden behind the booking counter. "And the pictures?"

Karen almost smirked as she handed him four stacks of eight by ten prints.

"That was quick. Thanks."

He handed Michelle and Sonny each a set. "Let's look."

When he was satisfied the prints were clear, he started through the stack again, giving each print closer study, trying to see it from the perspective of a juror.

He said, "look at number ten. Start from stake two and tell me what you see."

"Michelle?"

"Well, I see the stake you flagged. I see the ribbon leading from the stake to our presumed location for Gooding's body. Nothing else jumps out at me."

Sonny said, "I see what caught your eye, Boss. The pine needles. It's faint, but there appears to be a line from the stake to Gooding's body. Where the needles were turned over, the color is darker. I couldn't see it when I was on the ground, but it shows up in the photo."

"Like someone dragged Gooding from that location to the barnyard," Michelle added. "And tried to cover the drag marks by putting the needles back. It fits. It also gives us an idea of why Gooding's body was so far from the cane."

Bud was nodding. "I wonder what we might find if we rake some of those needles back?"

Sonny grabbed his Stetson. "I'm on it, Boss. Michelle, want to ride along?"

"I'd better go talk to those muddy-footed EMTs."

***

When he finished tagging the photos for the evidence file, Bud called Roger Hildebrand. Roger shared an office with Forest Service law enforcement officer Tom Johnson. Housed in the Paisley Ranger District, it was cheap rent, and Bud liked the idea that the two policemen could provide each other backup if it was needed.

"Good morning, Roger. How are you today?"

"Sonny called about half an hour ago. Told me about the Gooding mess. Sad business."

"It is." Bud paused and then said, "Anything going on in North County?"

"Yes, Oregon Department of Fish and Wildlife—aka 'moose and goose'—stopped in this morning. They're headed to Dairy Creek to look into some poaching. Some idiot has been shooting deer and then just leaving them.

"I also had to break up a fight at the Paisley Bar last night, and I wrote a Californian a ticket for doing about ninety-five past the Summer Lake Store. Don Wilson, who owns the store, called me. He was pissed as all get out.

"I caught our California friend on the straight stretch by the hot springs. I thought some about just scaring the crap out him and letting him go, but he got lippy, so I wrote him up."

"What was he driving?" Bud asked.

"He was in a silver BMW, and he was cooking. I think he was doing close to one ten, but I could only get a reading of ninety-five. I think he spotted me and was slowing down when I hit him with the radar. I doubt he'll actually pay the fine, but I figure the state police can worry about that. At least he was behaving himself when I let him go."

"What about the fight?"

"Oh, it wasn't much, just a cut lip and some hard cussing. Actually, it was funny. Georgia Blackmon was in there with some cowboy, when Wes, her husband, charged into the place and started calling her names that were less than flattering. The owner, Buffalo Boggs, called me. Anyway, before I got there Georgia slugged Wes—hit him a good one and knocked him down. She told him to quit following her around."

Bud laughed. "I'll bet he was a tad embarrassed."

"Old Wes had his tail between his legs and the tavern crowd was cracking up. He wasn't hurt too much, so I just told him to go on home."

"Is he the type to retaliate?"

"No. I've known him for years. He'll probably just kick her out again like he did last time. Then she'll sober up and beg him to take her back. And then he'll take her back again."

"Well, if she hits him again, arrest her for assault. I don't care if she is female."

"I'll tell her what you said. So, how you coming on the Gooding case?"

"I'll know better after the autopsy, but I'm convinced it wasn't an accident. I think somebody killed that old man, and I suspect they did it with a whiskey bottle. I don't know that for sure, and I don't know why.

"When we arrest Casey, we might know more. I'll keep you posted. Anything more on that meth lab in Christmas Valley?"

"I'm following up with the ranch hand who called me, but he's not there right now. Some guy who answered the phone said he would be back next week."

"Okay. By the way, what's Buffalo's real name?"

"I don't know. He won't say. When people ask him he just says that only Mama, God, the IRS, and his banker know and that's damned well too many. I suppose we could run a check, but hell, Bud, that would just spoil the fun. What if it really is Buffalo?"

***

Nancy Sixkiller called almost the moment he hung up. "Lake County Sheriff's Office," he answered.

"This is Nancy. I have a message from a Linda Blair."

"Cute," he said. "What's the message?"

"I think I should bring it over."

"Come on, tell me what she said."

"Well," Nancy said with a smile in her voice, "she said she wouldn't be coming down."

"That's it? No explanation?"

"Seems clear enough to me," Nancy answered.

"Hmmm...Well, thanks."

"Oh, you're very welcome, Mr. Sheriff. And Sonny called in. He's got a hot tip on the cattle rustling in Plush. Said he didn't know when he'd be back."

"I'd love to catch those bastards," he said. "Thanks, Nancy." He pondered a minute and then decided he really did want to know why Linda wasn't coming down. His ex-wife answered on the second ring.

"Linda? I got your message. What's up?"

"I'm embarrassed that I called you in the first place," she said in that husky voice that brought back so many memories. "I was hurting, I'm still hurting over Mom's death, but I've sort of caught my breath again. Bud, I don't want to hurt your feelings, but I don't think it's a good idea for me to come down. I'd love to see your cabin, but...I don't know. I don't think it's a good idea."

"You're probably right," he answered, and then just stopped talking.

"Thanks for calling, Bud. I've got to go. I'm meeting with Mom's lawyer in about an hour to go over the will."

He hung up without saying goodbye. Then he rocked back in his old captain's chair, clasped his hand behind his head, and with a grimace said quietly, "Yep, she's right. That was not one of my brighter ideas."

He was busy at a flip chart plotting out the progress in the investigation of Gordon Gooding's death when Michelle returned to the station.

Already taped to one wall was a timeline:
Estimated time of death: 1400-1600 Wednesday 4-12
911 call: 1615 (Franklin Pierce) 4-12
Arrival of EMTs: 1628 4-12
DOA Hospital: 1705 4-12

***

Through the front window, he watched the tall, slender deputy walk across the street and noted that she was smiling. And she was humming when she opened the door.

"Good trip?"

She blushed, and then with her chin jutting, said, "I just got asked out."

"Well, hell, I thought you had some information for me. We're trying to run a sheriff's department here in case you hadn't noticed. Okay, I'll bite. Who's the lucky fellow?"

"Charlie Prince," she said smugly.

"Good for you. He seems like a nice guy. A bit tall for me."

"Well, he's not asking you out either," she assured him. "And I did do some business." She handed him a copy of Chief Gus Hildebrand's report.

"The EMTs said Gordon Gooding was face down in the mud when they got there. And Chief Hildebrand's report substantiates that. The Chief handled the call himself, and his report says he was there about three minutes before the ambulance arrived. So the EMTs hadn't turned him over yet."

"Interesting. Did Gus interview Pierce?" He turned back to his timeline.

First officer to arrive: Approximately 1625 (Chief Hildebrand) 4-12

"That part is a bit sketchy, but Pierce was still there when the Chief arrived. The report says he was waiting by the bridge. Pierce told Chief Hildebrand that he found the body when he drove out to talk to Gooding about selling the ranch."

"Right. Now, look at this timeline. Suggest anything?"

"Well, we don't know very much yet."

"Yeah, but what if we knew when Casey called Pierce?"

"Well, we might at least know when Gooding was last alive?"

"Maybe. I'll get Karen to pull Casey's phone records. And would you mind checking with the County Library to see what they have on spiders?"

She looked at her watch. "I don't mind, but Amy Woodruff said I could talk to Melissa Casey again at 11:30. That gives me two hours to get to Klamath Falls."

Bud looked surprised. "They took her to Klamath Falls?"

"Yes, that's the closest facility. And they took her daughter Lucinda there too. I want to see what she might know as well."

"You'd better get going then. I guess I'll go to the library myself and see what I can find out about spiders."

"I thought you were going to contact County Extension?"

"Well, I thought I might do some reading before I called them."

He watched Michelle pull away in the Explorer and then called dispatch. The Colonel answered the phone. "This is Control."

"I'll be at the library. Do you have a location for Sonny?"

"He just called in. He was headed down Deep Creek canyon. We don't get very good reception down there, so he'll be out of touch for a few minutes. When he clears the canyon, we can contact him. Do you have a message for him?"

"Yes. Tell him to ask for backup if he gets…" Bud hesitated. "No, hell. Forget it. He knows his business."

"Worrying about your kids?"

"You know I am. It probably doesn't make good sense, but they work solo so much that I just naturally worry. If anything goes wrong, it can be a heck of a long time before they get any help."

"Yeah," the Colonel agreed. "It reminds me of fighting fire. No matter how well you trained the crews, or how much you trusted their judgment, you still worried. But you had to let them do the job."

Bud nodded his head into the phone, "Okay, Henry. You're right. I get the point. Anyway, I'll be at the library for a while."

"Got you covered, Sheriff."

***

Highway 140 follows Deep Creek as it flows east and threads a low rimmed canyon on its way to Warner Valley. The valley is walled on the east by Hart Mountain and on the west by the Warner Mountains.

Like its sisters, Abert Rim and Winter Rim, it is a high-in-the-sky fault scarp, a bit more eroded and broken, but still cliff-faced. In the valley, a series of land-locked lakes feed one into another north and out into the desert.

The water in the southern lakes—Pelican, Crump, and Hart—is freshened by several small streams, but as the water evaporates in the northern pools, the water becomes brackish and alkaline. In low water years the northern pools become crusted alkali planos.

Fish live in the fresh water of the southern lakes. And tens of thousands of migratory birds come each year in mid-March—some to stay, but most just resting and feeding before resuming the trip north. The arable land has been ditched and tilled by ranchers for pasture, hay, and grain.

Sonny slowed the county's pickup as he neared Adel, a white, single story, one-stop post office and store with gas pumps, café and a small area for a tavern.

Like a lot of old stage stops in the West, the living quarters were attached to the back of the building. A local ranch hand and his young wife lived in a fifty-foot single-wide trailer behind the store.

The wife worked part-time for the proprietor, Amy O'Fallon. Amy's husband had the good grace to drink himself to death before he impoverished them both.

Sonny pulled into the pumps, unlocked the cap to the tank, and inserted the nozzle from the diesel pump. Amy's thin Asian face appeared in the window, and she shook a finger at him.

Oregon was one of two states that still didn't permit self-service gas, but that was pretty much ignored in rural areas.

When he finished pumping the diesel and took the county credit card inside to pay, Amy scolded him. "You are a bad boy, Sonny Sixkiller. You are supposed to uphold the law, and there you go breaking it." She didn't smile, but there was amusement in her voice.

It was a familiar ritual, and Sonny smiled and said, "I guess you better turn me in, Amy."

"What are you doing in Adel, Mr. Sonny?"

He gave his belt an exaggerated hitch and said, "Well ma'am, it seems some outlaws have been terrorizing the neighbors, and I'm here to set 'em straight. They've got till noon, or else."

She laughed politely. "You are no John Wayne. You here about the cattle rustling."

"Yes ma'am, I am. I aim to set them straight too."

"It is a bad thing. People work hard and then some bad persons come along and take what the others work hard for. They steal part of a life. In Cambodia we would chop their heads off and send the head back to their relatives. But this is a stupid country about some things. You throw them in jail, they get out, do bad things again, you throw them in jail again. You bring them back here and I will chop their heads off."

"First, I have to catch them, Amy. And then I have to protect them from unkind citizens who have no mercy in their hearts."

"I'll show them mercy. You just bring them back to me. And you will catch them. Their truck broke down on Hogback Road."

"How did you find that out?"

"Lonny left about fifteen minutes ago with Chance to catch the bad men."

"Damn! That's not funny, Amy. If they shoot anybody they could be in worse trouble than the rustlers."

"I want them to shoot the bad men. You won't do it if you catch them first."

Sonny hit the flashers as he spun the pickup around and back to Hogback Road, turning north to Plush and the Rabbit Hills.

He was on the radio as soon as he settled down. "Control, this is County Two."

"Control. Go ahead."

"I'm headed north to Plush. I have a report of a cattle truck broken down on Hogback out in the Rabbit Hills. The locals believe it belongs to some cattle rustlers. I also have a report that two ranchers are in pursuit of the rustlers. The ranchers have a fifteen-minute head start on me."

"Copy."

"I'm thinking we need to intercept anyone coming out on the upper end of Hogback where it ties into 395. And I don't give a damn if it's ranchers or rustlers. If it's ranchers, have them arrested for interfering with an officer."

"Copy."

Sonny hung up the mic and concentrated on his driving. Top speed in the diesel was about ninety-five, but the narrow asphalt road wouldn't allow that anyway.

As his anger cooled, he slowed the pickup and settled into a more reasonable 65 mph and thought about the rustling. It wasn't very hard to do. Cut a fence. Run a few steers into a cattle truck in the middle of the night in the middle of nowhere. Wire the fence back together and take the steers to a dishonest butcher someplace else.

If the rustlers kept the truck on hard surfaces, asphalt or gravel, there were no tire tracks, and unless they used horses to herd the steers into the truck, there was little to go on except maybe some boot prints.

The only telltale might be a concentration of steer manure on the road. It could be days or weeks before the rancher decided someone had taken some of his stock. By then, the rustlers could be in another state.

The radio squawked. Sonny recognized Nancy's voice. "County Two, this is Control."

He picked up the mic. "This is County Two."

"County One, County Three, and Trooper Prince are headed to the junction of 395 and Hogback. ETA is twenty minutes. Another State trooper will sweep 395 from Riley Junction to Hogback.

And Bud says to stay back until you have some support. If you catch up to them, just herd them along."

"Now what in the hell does that mean?"

"It means, don't get hurt."

He slowed down to fifty as he passed the trading post in Plush, another old stage stop that had become the anything/everything mini-mart, post office, and gas station.

Old Mrs. Mitchell was standing out front and waved as he drove through. He honked and waved back. By this time, everyone in the Warner Valley probably had the word that the "posse" was in hot pursuit, presumably hot on the trail of the rustlers that had been stealing steers with impunity for the past couple of years. He could almost hear her saying, "Go get 'em." Or more likely, "Shoot the sons-of-bitches."

Spring green-up was showing in the pastures near Plush, but as he pushed the pickup on up Hogback, the pastures gave way to stunted sage and rabbit brush. The pavement turned to gravel at the little strip known as the airport.

Three miles further on, Sonny got his first break. The Callahan brothers, Lonnie and Chance, were going too fast to negotiate a left-hand corner where Hogback turned to parallel a fence line.

They were both standing in the road beside an older brown GMC 4x4. Sonny could see strips of mud where they had been spinning the tires trying to drive the pickup out of the ditch. Stuck they were, and stuck they'd stay if Sonny had anything to do with it.

Lights still flashing, Sonny slid to a stop and powered down the passenger side window. Lonnie, the taller of the two brothers, was a lean, sun-browned six-footer about twenty-five years old. He took off a stained, black Stetson, leaned in the window, and said, "We slid off the road. Pull us out. We're going with you." His tone was angry and belligerent.

Sonny just looked at Lonnie for a few seconds, and then laughed. "Hell, Amy O'Fallon has first dibs on the rustlers. She said she's going to cut their heads off. So I just can't let you come along and shoot them and spoil her fun."

"By God, we're coming with you."

"No, and I'm not calling for a wrecker either. You two can damn well dig out your pickup or walk back to Plush. Maybe you'll be cooled down by then."

Sonny's dark eyes turned hard and flat. "If you two ever interfere with any of my cases again, I'll arrest you, I'll cuff you and I'll take you to town for a couple of the most uncomfortable nights you've ever had. Understood?"

Lonnie took a step back from the window. Finally he said, "Damn, Sonny. We just thought we had a shot at those guys. They've been robbing us blind."

"I know, and I hope to catch them, arrest them, cuff them and take them back to town for years of uncomfortable nights, not just the couple I'm willing to give you. Comprende?"

Sonny put the transmission back in gear. "I've got to go. We have a couple of officers waiting at the highway for these dudes, assuming they haven't gotten away completely."

"We want to come with you."

"Can't. It's against company policy to get civilians shot, or to let them shoot other civilians."

With a gravel throwing start, Sonny left them standing there beside their mud-bound vehicle. When the road veered to the northwest and started its long, gentle climb out of the basin, Sonny eased off the gas pedal to let a running jackrabbit cross the road, then sped up again. He spotted a lone antelope standing on a low ridge about half a mile off the road. Then he spotted the truck about a half-mile ahead up the long, straight road. It wasn't moving.

Sonny killed the emergency warning lights and slowed. About two hundred yards from the truck, he stopped. With a pair of ten-by binoculars, he studied the vehicle.

It looked to be a faded blue horse-van mounted on a two-ton farm truck. The loading ramp was down and the passenger side door was open. He couldn't see any movement, but he could see four white-faced steers feeding out in the sagebrush about four or five hundred yards to his right. Sonny reached back in the pickup and unclipped the mic.

"Control, this is County Two."

Nancy came back immediately. "This is Control. I read you, County Two."

"I'm about two hundred yards from a stock truck. It's parked on the side of Hogback, approximately six miles northwest of the junction of Hogback and the Flagstaff Lake Road. I can't see any movement or signs of anybody near the truck. I see four steers out in the sagebrush, and no one runs cattle out here this time of year."

"Say again County Two. County One can read you, but it's garbled."

"I said I found the suspect vehicle, a farm truck with a stock van mounted on it, about six miles northwest of the junction of Hogback Road and Flagstaff Lake Road. I'm also seeing some steers where there shouldn't be any. The truck appears to be deserted and the loading ramp is down."

"County One. Control. Did you copy that?" The squelch broke on Sonny's radio, but he couldn't make out the conversation. Nancy's voice broke in. "That's right, six miles northwest of the junction of Hogback Road and Flagstaff Lake Road. Okay. Copy."

"County Two, County One asks you to stay where you are and block Hogback. Don't let anyone go by you. They're about ten minutes from the junction of 395 and Hogback. They'll start a sweep towards you. And you should be able to read County One when he gets to the north end of Abert Lake. He'll call to let you know when he's in position. Meantime, sit tight."

"I can do that. County Two, clear."

"Control, clear."

Sonny shut the motor off, put his brown Stetson on the seat, and slipped his personal portable into a leather case on his left hip. He adjusted the volume and squelch and then fastened the lapel mic in place. He unsnapped the holster on his .357 magnum and eased out into the sagebrush.

Other officers carried the .40 caliber Glock, but Sonny was never quite comfortable with the thought of a jammed cartridge during a confrontation; he preferred the more dependable revolver.

He used a low hummock about seven or eight feet high to cover his movements, even though he knew full anyone with a lick of sense would know a police vehicle was blocking the road. But he wanted a better view of the cab of the truck.

When he was about two hundred yards to the right of his pickup, he eased up the short slope behind the tallest sagebrush he could find and got down in the short cheat grass to glass the truck. The sun was warm on his back. One steer looked in his direction and then went back to grazing.

Patiently, he conducted a systematic visual search of the area. He could see part of the interior of the cab through the open passenger door. Nothing was visible. Unless someone was lying down in the seat, the cab looked empty. He tried to concentrate, but in his heart he knew the truck was deserted. Bud had told him to sit tight, so that's what he was doing. His mind drifted to thoughts of Carol Connor.

Last Friday night he'd taken her to the Alger movie theater, which opened on Friday, Saturday, and Sunday nights…usually. They tried to sit through "Blackhawk Down," but after about forty-five minutes Carol squeezed his hand and nodded to leave. When they were on the street she said, "It's too bloody, sad, and depressing." They walked the three blocks to the Indian Village and had a drink in the bar. The bar crowd thought they made a good-looking couple.

They had started seeing each other casually about a year ago, after the senior high school class asked them, independently, to chaperone the junior/senior prom.

The prom committee had argued reasonably enough that parents would feel better if a policeman was there to chaperone. And the truth was that more than one high school girl had a crush on the good-looking deputy.

One devious child decided that if she couldn't have him, then maybe the pretty, but single, Miss Connor should. So, quite unaware, Carol and Sonny had been kindly and deviously manipulated.

Out of boredom with the prom and some curiosity about the pretty young woman in the black, form-fitting dress, Sonny asked Carol to dance. They had been keeping company on a regular basis ever since.

Somewhere in the rock bottom of his soul, Sonny knew with certainty he was going to marry Carol. And with just as much certainty, he believed she knew it as well. For one thing, they talked. They talked about everything, and he was always astonished when he found himself talking to her about how he felt.

Talking about feelings just wasn't done when he was growing up. It wasn't because of his Indian upbringing. His grandfather was an open person who easily shared his feelings with his family. It was his father. Something happened to his father in Vietnam that stoppered his feelings, something which made him distrust any display of emotion.

When Sonny found himself telling Carol about how he felt about life and about her, he was always a little embarrassed. He told her that too.

She scolded him gently for shying away from his feelings, and then said, "We're all the victims of our parents. Remember, they were just youngsters when they were raising us. But at some point we all have to take charge. You can't blame your parents beyond that point anymore."

Bud's voice on the radio snapped him back to the present. "County Two, we're at the junction of 395 and Hogback."

Sonny looked at his watch. He'd been daydreaming and going through the motions of surveillance for over twenty minutes. Good thing the bad guys had left the scene. "This is County Two. I copy."

"We're headed your way."

"You know, I've been watching that truck for over twenty minutes. They aren't here. I've got a hunch they unloaded the steers and then rode out on horseback. So keep an eye open for tracks. Given the route they took to get in here, I think they planned to head north up 395 with these steers."

"Can you see the plates well enough to get a number?"

"No. The rear of the truck is pretty dirty."

"Okay. Just sit tight."

Sonny heard a vehicle behind him coming slowly from the direction of Plush. He could hear the rumble of a diesel engine and the crunch of gravel under the tires. It was a big Ford F350 pulling a gooseneck stock trailer. The driver stopped about fifty yards from Sonny's pickup and got out. Sonny recognized the lanky figure of Leonard Callahan.

"At least he didn't bring Lonnie and Chance with him," Sonny muttered under his breath.

He slipped back below the crest of the low ridge and waved to let Callahan know where he was, then waved him to get back. Callahan got back in the truck, started the engine, backed down the road another hundred yards, and stopped again.

This time Callahan turned the engine off and just sat in the cab and waited.

Twenty minutes later, Sonny saw the Sheriff's white pickup easing slowly down the road, Trooper Prince following in his black-and-white. There was about a twenty-yard interval between the vehicles.

When the sheriff was about a hundred yards from the stock truck, he stopped, and Trooper Prince closed up behind him. Bud's voice came on the radio. "We're in place. Let's go check it out."

"Give me a minute," Sonny said. "I've got Leonard Callahan parked down the road. Let me go tell him what's going on."

When Sonny stepped out on the gravel, he waved Callahan forward. Callahan fired up the diesel and eased on up the road to where Sonny waited.

"Morning, Mr. Callahan."

"Morning, Sonny."

"I'm glad you didn't bring Lonnie or Chance."

Callahan gave him a wry smile. "No, I didn't think that was such a good idea. When they told me you left them afoot, I figured you did the right thing. By now they're just about halfway to Plush still cussin' their daddy. Dispatch told me you found some steers."

Sonny pointed to the north. "I think that little bunch out in the sagebrush might be yours.

"So, here's what's going to happen. I think the rustlers are long-gone, but in this business it doesn't pay to take chances. I'm going to move my rig on up the road. When I get about fifty yards from that truck up there, I'm going to stop, and my shotgun and I are going to check the vehicle for bad guys.

"Roger's going to slip out into the sagebrush with his rifle and sniper scope to cover us. The sheriff and Trooper Prince are going to come on down the road, and then they're going to approach the vehicle on foot from an angle on each side of the vehicle. That way we stand less chance of shooting each other.

"In the meantime, Leonard, you sit tight. When it's safe, I'll wave you on in." Sonny glanced at the thirty-thirty lever-action Winchester in a rack behind Callahan. "And please don't get any ideas about playing hero."

Sonny approached to within about sixty yards of the rear of the rustler's truck, and then, shotgun in hand, he stepped out of the pickup and spoke quietly into his mic. "I'm in place."

Even though he was convinced the truck was empty, he was still hyper alert. He watched Roger take position on a small rise left of the truck to provide cover. Then he started his approach.

Bud was coming in from Sonny's right, with Trooper Prince coming in at an angle on the left. He was glad to see they were wearing their body armor. He was close enough to see into the van box. "The back is empty," he hollered.

The rest was anticlimactic. When the sheriff was crouched behind the right front fender of the truck, Sonny moved up alongside, near the open passenger door.

"All right," Bud hollered, "come on out!" Nobody did, of course.

Trooper Prince jerked the driver's door open. "Empty."

They each took a deep breath. Charlie holstered his Glock. Bud and Sonny each slid the safety back on their shotguns. Roger came on in to the cattle truck. Sonny said, "Hell, Bud, you sounded like something out of the movies." They all broke into laughter.

Sonny waved Callahan on up the road. The four officers started a systematic search of the vehicle. The cab was filled with a wealth of empty biscuit-sized Copenhagen cans, candy wrappers, beer cans, a roach clip in the ashtray, a stray .22 caliber round, and two shiny .308 caliber rounds. One more was on the ground on the passenger side of the truck.

"Damn," Roger said, "the bastards have a .308 rifle."

"I think I'd better let Trooper Hansen know," Charlie said and started for his patrol car. "He's the one coming down 395 from Riley."

Callahan pulled up behind Sonny's pickup and got out. Bud met him at the back of the truck. "Leonard, I'd appreciate it if you didn't walk around the truck much until we finish here."

"What did you find?"

"Well," Bud said, "a lot of trash we can probably lift some prints from. Fresh mud on the floor mats, both sides, which tells us there were at least two people in the truck. Some brand new, shiny .308 rounds, one on the ground, and that suggests at least one of those idiots has a rifle. Some evidence of pot smoking and the tracks of one horse headed on up the road. As soon as you verify the brands on those steers, we should know they were stolen. And I can tell you right now we have a clear-cut case of the stupids."

Roger walked back to where Bud was talking to Callahan. "I found the registration in the glove box. The truck is registered to a Walter C. Johannsen with a Riley address."

"I know Walt," Callahan said. "He has a ranch on Silver Creek. Hell, he wouldn't rustle cattle. I've known him for years."

"We're still going to have to talk to him, but you're probably right, Leonard."

"Okay, Sonny," Bud said, "give me a theory about this boondoggle."

"As I see it, our rustlers cut a fence somewhere and loaded the steers in the truck sometime last night. Then they drove to here. The truck broke down or they ran out of gas. Either way, they panicked, offloaded the steers and one horse." He pointed at the single set of horse tracks. "Then they decided to ride the horse out of here."

"Make a guess as to the time?"

"Okay, most people go to bed pretty early. So, to give themselves time to get out of the country..."

Leonard interrupted. "I can do better than that. Ida Mitchell, the old gal who runs the store in Plush, said she heard a truck go through about quarter after midnight last night. Said it was traveling north."

"Then say the truck broke down about 12:30," Sonny theorized. "Allow five minutes to turn the steers loose, offload the horse, and grab what you can from the cab. That gives them about twelve hours. How far can a horse travel in twelve hours, Leonard?"

"It depends on the horse, the men, and whether they stuck to the roads or went across country. If they stuck to the road and did a tie and ride, they could average five miles an hour."

"Sixty miles?" Bud asked incredulously.

"Like I said, it depends on the horse and the men."

Roger had been listening, which was quite a chore for Roger since he liked to yarn so much. "You know, what I'm thinking is that a couple of cowhands borrowed their boss's truck while he was off someplace, probably the same cowhands that've been rustling all along. Then this junk heap breaks down and the game's over."

"Well," Bud said, "I'll tell you what we're going to do about it. We're going to have this truck towed to our yard in Lakeview. We're going to find some fingerprints. The fingerprints are going to identify the people who were in this truck. And then we are going to issue some arrest warrants. I'll be damned if I'm going to chase them across country."

Sonny said, "Leonard, I want to get some pictures of the truck and especially the tracks of those steers. It's pretty obvious they were hauled here and then unloaded. Then you can help us best by rounding up your steers.

"I'm also wondering if you could get those boys of yours to ride the fences and find where the rustlers cut it. You can bet it'll be close to a road. If it looks like someone used fresh wire to splice the fence, I want that wire. We can run a spectrographic analysis and we might have one more piece of evidence."

Charlie came back from his black-and-white, walking hurriedly. He started talking before he got to them. "A rancher flagged down Trooper Hansen near Alkali Lake. The rancher said someone stole his pickup last night and left a strange horse in the pasture. It wasn't hard to steal the pickup because those people out there always leave the keys in the ignition. Hansen said he was headed back to Riley to check on the Johannsen place."

"There we go," Bud said. "Let's get this outfit towed back to town. Sonny, I hate to ask you this, but would you stay with the truck until the wrecker gets here?"

"Not a problem, Boss. I already called it in. And I'll help Leonard load his steers."

"And I'll give you a hand," Roger added.

Bud turned to Charlie. "Charlie, I am grateful for your assistance."

"Anytime, Sheriff. I always enjoy a good party."

"Thanks." Bud walked back to his pickup to use his radio. "Control. County One."

"Control. Go ahead."

"Everything's in hand here. The rustlers abandoned their truck, turned the steers loose, and took off on horseback. I think they may have stolen a truck and headed towards Riley. Did you copy Charlie's message to Hansen?"

"Yes. We've contacted the Sheriff's office in Burns. They said they would tie in with Trooper Hansen for a check of the Johannsen place."

"Good. County One, clear."

CHAPTER 7

Michele Trivoli stopped at a Mini Mart on the edge of town and asked for directions to Kingsley Air Base. The attendant didn't know, but he was willing to sell her a nice Klamath Falls street map. She parted with four one-dollar bills and took the map to her vehicle to plot a route to Kingsley. She suspected the Mini Mart sold lots of city street maps.

She pulled into the Safeway parking lot and glared at a robust man who pulled into the handicapped parking and ran into the store. He did have a handicapped sticker in the window.

"They must hand those out as door prizes," she muttered. Inside she chose a bright, colorful, mixed bouquet of cut flowers and paid the clerk.

The office of KCBRA, the Klamath County Battering and Rape Alliance, generally referred to as "KOBRA," was in a barracks complex inside a ten-foot cyclone fence which surrounded the air base.

An airman in camo, carrying a side arm and a clipboard, flagged Michelle down at the gate. A second airman carrying an M16 was standing behind a sandbagged revetment. Even though her vehicle was clearly marked, she still had to produce her badge and explain the purpose of her visit.

The airman checked his clipboard. "Yes, ma'am. You're expected. Turn right at the first corner. The second barracks on the left is the one you want." He raised the steel barrier pole and Michelle drove through a tight S-shaped entry flanked by tiger teeth and concrete tank traps. They were positioned to force any vehicle entering the base to negotiate two very tight corners.

I guess if I wanted a place where I could feel safe, this would work as well as any, Michelle thought.

There was no sign in front of the two-story, concrete block barracks. But it wasn't hard to tell which one was used by KOBRA. There were freshly tilled flowerbeds planted to red, white and purple spring petunias.

She pushed a buzzer, and a pleasant, smiling woman of about forty with short curly dark hair peeked through a side window. A buzz sounded and Michelle pulled the door open.

"Hi. I'm Carrie West. We've been expecting you." She held out her hand.

Michelle shook hands. "I'm Michelle Trivoli."

Carrie West led Michelle down a narrow hallway past a series of regularly spaced doors that had once been barracks rooms.

Melissa Casey was propped up in a hospital bed complete with a summons button to call for help. A young woman with tired eyes was setting a cup of tea on the meal cart tray. She turned, and her eyes reflected a momentary panic as she saw the uniform. And just as quickly it passed.

Just habit, Michelle thought.

"Hello, Melissa. I brought these for you." She held out the bouquet.

Melissa had two black eyes and her lips were still swollen. She winced with pain as she reached out to take Michelle's bouquet. "Hi. This is my friend Rhonda. She's been looking after me. Thank you for the flowers."

"Hello, Rhonda. I'm glad Melissa has someone to look out for her. Are you on the staff here?"

Rhonda shook her head. "No, I've been here about three weeks, my baby and me. Carrie's helping me look for work and taking care of the legal stuff for me."

"I see."

"I was just telling Melissa how guilty I felt when I called the cops on my old man. But the KOBRA staff has helped me see that I wasn't the problem. Oh, I mean, I still feel like I was partly to blame, but it ain't okay to beat on people." She hesitated.

"Especially babies. I've been talking to Melissa, trying to get her to tell you it was her husband that beat her up. I mean, she needs to get pissed about it."

Michelle glanced at Melissa. There were tears forming in Melissa's eyes. She squeezed her eyes shut and starting whispering.

"What are you saying, Melissa? Please?"

"Oh, God!" she wailed. "He killed that old man and beat me... bad this time."

Michelle stopped stock still, and then set the flowers on the meal cart. "Melissa, he won't hurt you anymore. I promise. And this is important. So please answer me. Did he say he killed Mr. Gooding?"

"Oh, Lord. What's going to happen to Lucinda and me? He killed that old man, he told me he did. And then he got drunk, and after Lucinda left for school he started shouting and hitting me. And then he threw a gun and some camping gear in the pickup and tore out of there." She was crying and trembling and her new friend Rhonda was patting her arm and trying to comfort her.

Carrie West touched Michelle's sleeve and said, "Wouldn't you like to come to my office and have a cup of coffee?"

When she was seated in Carrie's office holding a cup of coffee, Michelle said, "I feel awful to put her through this, but it has to be reported. And I'd like a statement from you. The part about her husband beating her is admissible as evidence. The second part could be challenged as hearsay, second-hand information, but it's enough to put out a warrant for Casey's arrest for murder."

Carrie leaned back in her swivel chair, sipped the coffee, and studied Michelle. "She'll have to testify to the beating. Will she have to testify about her husband saying he killed that old man?"

"That's up to the DA, but I can't see any way around it."

"I've been in the mental health business for almost eighteen years, so I am here to tell you this. She's very fragile right now, and she's likely to retract what she just said. At some later date when she has the support she needs, and when she learns that what happened isn't her fault, she may be willing to testify. But it takes time and lots of healing and support before she'll be ready for that. Her physical scars will heal, but the emotional scars may never heal. Only time and patience can help her."

Michelle nodded and changed the subject. "How is Lucinda holding up?"

"Actually, she seems relieved to be someplace safe. Will you need to interview her?"

"After what Melissa just told us, I don't think that will be necessary."

"Good. She's gone through quite a lot."

Michelle just nodded her head. "I believe you, but I still don't understand how a husband could do this!" She hesitated, got herself under control. She pulled her cell phone from a jacket pocket and said, "Mrs. West, I need to call my boss."

***

Karen Highsmith answered the sheriff's phone. "Lake County Sheriff's Office."

"Karen, this is Michelle. I'm in Klamath Falls. I just interviewed Melissa Casey. Two things: First, Mrs. Casey told me and two—no, make that one—reliable witness that William Casey beat her. Second, she says he told her he killed Gordon Gooding. So we should update the APB on Casey to 'Wanted in connection with a homicide.'"

"I can see to that. Right now the whole crew is up north rounding up some rustlers, but I'll relay your message."

"Good. I'll be here a while longer taking a statement from one of the witnesses. I'll try to get a written statement from Melissa

Casey, but I'm told not to be surprised if she recants. Would you patch me through to dispatch?"

Nancy Sixkiller answered and said, "Hold please, just a minute." In the background Michelle could hear a radio message clearly enough to recognize Bud's voice.

While she waited, her thoughts drifted to another, smaller mystery. She noticed that Nancy's tone of voice always seemed to soften a bit when she talked to Bud. And once she caught Bud watching Nancy in that speculative way men have when they are attracted to a woman. Why didn't they at least date? Have dinner, go to a movie…something?

"Michelle, you still there?"

"Yes. Go ahead."

"Bud said to tell you 'good job,' and to get back to Lakeview ASAP with the statements. And by the way, they just found an abandoned cattle truck that was used by rustlers to steal some cattle."

"That's good news. Okay, I should be back there by about six o'clock."

"Take your time and drive carefully." Nancy hung up.

Michelle placed the handset back into the cradle of the phone. "Carrie, I have to get some statement forms from my rig, but I'll be right back."

"Michelle, I know you're on official business, and I know you're in a hurry, but what would you say to some lunch? I know a good pizza place that has a salad bar and other 'good for you' food. We can find a booth in the back, and I'll write out my statement while you eat."

"I need to at least try for a statement from Melissa."

"That'll keep until after lunch. In fact, it might go better for Melissa after lunch as well."

"Okay. It's a deal."

***

It was closer to 7:30 p.m. than 6:30 when Michelle backed into a parking spot in front of the Sheriff's Office in Lakeview. The interview with Melissa Casey had been far from routine, and Michelle found herself being counseled by Carrie West. But now she had a statement from Melissa that her husband had beaten her and that he'd said he killed Gordon Gooding. Carrie West signed a statement that Melissa Casey said her husband had beaten her and that he killed Gordon Gooding.

In addition to the statements, Michelle had a stack of articles and half dozen books about the psychology of spousal abuse Carrie had loaned her. Murder she could understand…after a fashion. But the subject of spousal abuse had fastened on her mind. She couldn't shake it. And she damned well didn't understand it.

Bud was on the phone, and the district attorney, Howard Finch, was sitting in Michelle's swivel chair hunched over a form of some kind and scribbling away when she walked in. Bud was animated, and his eyes were bright.

Bud said, "Okay! Thanks. We'll meet Tom Johnson and Roger Hildebrand at the Warner Ski Lodge at oh five hundred."

"Howdy, stranger," Bud said as she walked in and dumped her canvas carryall on a desk. "Good trip?"

"I'm pooped. It wasn't the drive over there and back so much as it was talking to Melissa Casey. But I did get a statement from her and from Carrie West, the director of Cobra, so it was worth the trip."

Howard's baritone boomed, "Let me see." He took the two statements.

While Howard read, Michelle noted an addition to Bud's timeline.

- Phone call from Casey to Pierce: 1330

When Howard finished reading the statements, Michelle said, "I haven't had time to write my report."

Tapping the papers with a pudgy forefinger, Howard declared, "These are good enough for now."

"Nice job," Bud said.

"So…what's going on?"

"Well," Bud started in, "a fellow from the Forest Service spotted fresh tire tracks on an old road running into that country south of Drake Peak, and he got curious. So, he followed them in and found Casey's pickup stuck in a snowdrift. You know how those snowdrifts get this time of year, crusted on top and hollow underneath. Anyway, Casey must have driven up on top of the snowdrift and broken through. Got himself stuck, he did. Dale Breon, the Forest Service guy, called his dispatch center, who called us. There's an old shack up in there the hunters use. We surmise Casey is, or at least might be, hiding there. So, in the morning we're going to intrude upon his solitude.

"Sonny's out now finding us some horses to use. The Forest Service has three we can borrow, so all we need are three more. I'm headed over to the interagency dispatch to look at some maps. The Lakeview district ranger and her fire management officer are going to meet us there in about fifteen minutes."

The phone rang. Bud answered, "Sheriff's Office." He listened for a few seconds and then said, "Good, Roger. We'll see you at the Warner Ski Lodge at 0500. Yeah, thanks."

He hit zero for dispatch. "Nancy, call Sonny and tell him Roger has the horses we'll need in the morning. And get ahold of Charlie Prince for me. Ask him if he can meet us at the interagency dispatch center." He paused and then said, " Yeah, I will, Nancy. I always wear warm clothes and my body armor. Okay, ma'am. Yes, ma'am, I'll take a weapon. Just call Charlie."

He turned and looked first at Warren and then at Michelle. "You know, sometimes that woman reminds of my mother."

"Or a wife," Michelle said quietly.

"I heard that," Bud said.

Howard Finch roared with laughter, and Michelle smiled while Bud just turned red and glared at them. Finally, he gave them a sheepish grin. "Oh hell, she mothers everybody."

Howard spoke up. "These statements are sufficient to issue an arrest warrant for murder and aggravated assault. I still haven't seen the autopsy report, but I'm betting the autopsy and the physical evidence you've gathered will support the charge. And you all be careful. I know Casey. He's a drunk, and he's going to be desperate."

"By the way," he continued, "your buddy Franklin Pierce Junior is dragging his feet on Gooding's bank records. If he doesn't produce the records by ten tomorrow morning, I'm going to have him arrested for obstruction of justice, that asshole."

"Judas priest, Howard! We'll all be in the brush tomorrow morning. I can't take time out to arrest Pierce."

"I know that. I'll have the City arrest him and throw him in your fine jail."

Bud paused. "Howard, thanks."

"Well, I know this much," Howard said. "You're keeping my office busy. Hell, you might even get me re-elected." And then he laughed.

Patty Allison, Lakeview District Ranger; James "Doc" Holliday, fire management officer; and Dale Breon were waiting at the interagency fire dispatch center when Bud, Sonny, and Michelle arrived. The Feds were in Forest Service greens, complete with name tags and badges.

Patty, a petite blond, waved them over to a huge plastic-covered wall map that displayed the Fremont National Forest and all of the Bureau of Land Management and State of Oregon lands in Lake and Klamath counties. They formed a half circle in front of the map while two dispatchers watched from their chairs.

Dale showed them on the map where the pickup had been found and approximately where the cabin was located. "If you go out the Warner Highway about nine miles, there's an old road that runs north onto the flanks of Drake Peak. I make it to be about three and a half miles in to the cabin. There's another old road off the Drake Peak road that comes around the southwest flank of the mountain. It's not used much except during deer season, and there's a locked gate where the road enters the private land in there.

"Now there's another old track that comes in from the east on the Plush side of things. But that's not usable this time of year. The cabin—I've been in there during deer season because we have a right-of-way for fire access—sits in a small grove of bull pine. It's pretty brushy in there, so you can't really see the cabin until you're right up to it."

Bud studied the map. "Can you get to the Drake Peak road this time of year?"

Doc answered. "Not unless we plow snow. We don't generally get into that country until late May. And we still have to plow the snow here and there. It's funny country. I've found big, shaded snowbanks across the road until mid-June. Once we open them up, they just melt away."

"What about foot travel?" Sonny asked.

"Yeah, you can travel through there on foot. But where would you go?"

Patty handed them all a fairly detailed map that showed contours, stream courses, roads, and the position of the cabin her GIS group had run earlier. The scale was two inches to the mile. "Thanks," Bud said. "That's good detail. Better than anything we have. Is there someplace along the lower road we can unload our horses?"

Doc looked at Dale. Dale nodded and said, "Right after you turn off the highway there's a scab rock flat. That's big enough, and I think it's rocky enough that you won't bog down."

Patty asked, "How can we help?"

CHAPTER 8

Franklin Pierce was fairly quivering with indignation at the thought of being ordered by that twerp, that interloper Howard Finch to produce the Gooding records.

He sat dwarfed behind his daddy's big old teak desk and went over the bank statements for Gooding's savings and checking accounts, looking for something that might give the game away. The loan was the one chink in his armor. But then, banks do loan money, don't they? The only problem was Pierce had personally loaned Gooding the $35,000, not the bank.

This created a small ethical problem, but as vice president, he could always claim the bank would not have made the loan, so out of compassion he had personally underwritten it, thereby keeping the bank safe from a high-risk venture.

It didn't occur to Pierce that people who knew him would never describe him as compassionate. What they might say, however, was that he had used his position as an officer of the bank to broker the loan back to himself and pay the bank a miniscule interest rate for the privilege.

But he'd wanted this deal for himself. After years of being under his mother's thumb, he saw a way out. He ached to kiss the bank goodbye, to tell his mother at long last to "Kiss my ass," and to tell his nagging, bitch of a wife to go screw herself. It was time for some respect from the community.

Wealth! That was the answer, and the Gooding ranch was his key to wealth. The thought of actually leaving the area and starting over never entered his mind. They owed him a long, bitter debt and he was going to make sure they paid.

In his mind "they" were everyone except Susan McDowell.

Oh, he had learned to be sociable and friendly. The bank sponsored a Little League baseball team and bought a prize-winning lamb or steer from some 4-H kid at the county fair. But that was his protective camouflage.

It wasn't until he met, wooed, and bedded Susan McDowell that he began to like his life a little. She gave him love and the courage to dream. And the world he dreamed of wasn't the one he lived. He often worked after hours, telling his wife that the press of business would make him late. Or he managed to find a good training or conference out of town that even his mother couldn't argue with. And he managed to sneak Susan away with him when he did.

***

Like most clandestine romances, it started after Susan had come to work as a teller in the bank. Growing up in a family where chaos and uncertainty were the norm, she longed for a precise, controlled existence with few unknowns, a world where she was in control. Banking offered her that.

Numbers always added to a precise figure that could be verified. The hours were predictable. Banks were stable. After all, they had all the money. She liked computers for the same reason. Exactitude.

Susan was also a thief. More precisely, she was a skilled embezzler. And when she discovered some two years earlier that Mr. Pierce was embezzling from his own bank, her heart was touched and her passion ignited.

But Franklin was an inept thief, so Susan decided to teach him the fine art of computer banking. She waited until a warm summer evening when he was "working late" again, a common occurrence bank employees speculated as his way to delay going home to face an unhappy wife or his domineering mother.

Susan worked late that evening, too, muttering something about "auditing" to her boss, John North. North, a senior teller and one of the bank's three loan officers, hadn't thought anything about it and said, "All right. See you in the morning. My son's swim meet starts in fifteen minutes."

She knocked firmly on Franklin Pierce Junior's door and entered his office without waiting for an invitation. At five feet two, she was almost tiny, but she had a full figure, a clear complexion, and long brown hair. Her blue eyes were smiling as she laid two files on Franklin's desk.

"Mr. Pierce, you're an embezzler, and not a very good one."

His face blanched and he stuttered, "You…you…don't know what you're talking about."

She walked around the desk and opened the two files. One was the file of the loan the bank had made; the other was the file of the loan the borrower thought he had made. The discrepancy was a full two percent on a thirty-year home mortgage.

"You have the right idea," she said as she smiled at him, "but you're clumsy and you need some help. Now here's what we are going to do. First, you're going to correct this…let's call it…a mistake. I'll help you do that. No one will ever know there was a 'discrepancy.' Then we're going to start again, my way."

When he had recovered from his shock, and when it finally dawned on him that he wasn't going to jail, he started to speak. "Susan…"

"Miss McDowell," she interrupted. "You will always call me Miss McDowell, and I will always call you Mr. Pierce. Even in private. Understood?" And she smiled at him and caressed his cheek.

Their partnership was consummated on the expensive plush carpet in the office of Mr. Pierce. The stern portrait of the senior Franklin Pierce did nothing to dampen the enthusiasm of the moment.

CHAPTER 9

SMOKE WAS RISING from the fireplace chimney of the Warner Canyon Ski Lodge when Bud pull off the highway into the parking lot. It was 0500, or "oh dark of dawn," as Roger Hildebrand called it. Two green Forest Service pickups and two Lake County Sheriff's Department vehicles each with attached horse trailers were already parked alongside the lodge.

As Bud stepped out of his rig, Trooper Prince's cruiser turned off the highway and rolled quietly up beside him. Trooper Prince killed his headlights and uncoiled himself from the front seat.

"Morning, Bud," he said as he closed the car door. "Chilly this morning."

"Charlie. It is. I'm glad I wore my long johns."

"Maybe the cold will keep our fugitive in bed for a while."

"I hope so. I'd rather wake him up than find him up and waiting."

A quiet murmur of voices filled the chilly day-room. Roger, Sonny, Michelle, Pat Allison, and Dale Breon were standing in a semi-circle in front of the big fireplace, hands outstretched to the first flames of the log fire.

The Colonel and Tom Johnson, the Forest Service law enforcement officer from Paisley, were off to one side setting up two flip charts and a map board.

Chief Gus Hildebrand pushed through the door after Bud and Charlie.

"Damn, it's cold out there," Gus said. "Where's the coffee?" Patty Allison answered. "Good morning, Chief. There's a thermos over on the sideboard. And there's some really fine Styrofoam china. Help yourself. And put your empties in the recycle bin, please."

Gus grinned and said, "I don't suppose you remembered donuts."

"No. Did you?"

"As a matter of fact..." and he set a white baker's bag on the sideboard. Coffee in one hand and a glazed donut in the other, Gus eased his chunky body into the circle around the fireplace. "Are we getting warm or keeping the fire warm?" That brought the expected chuckle.

Bud appreciated Gus's presence. The light tone eased the tension a bit. At least it eased Bud's. "Okay everybody," he said. "Gather 'round." He started handing out a flyer. "This is a picture of Casey, and Dale is going to brief us on the location. Has anybody else ever been to the cabin?" A chorus of no's answered him.

Dale stood beside the map board. "About three miles east of here an old access road connects with the main highway. The access road runs pretty true to the north for about three-quarters of a mile and then veers to the northwest. The road crosses a small drainage right at this point." He stabbed the map with a forefinger. "It's a fairly deep cut and tough to drive across even in dry weather. That's where the pickup is stuck. There's a snowdrift across the drainage and the melt water undercut the drift. When he drove up on it, it caved in and dropped the front-end of his rig into that cut. The vehicle is definitely stuck.

"Anyway, about another three-quarters of mile further on, another dirt track intersects this one. It runs east to northeast for about a mile and a half to an old cabin. In dry weather, you can actually drive east on out to the Plush highway. The sheriff asked me to sketch the layout of the cabin, so if you'll look at the flip chart, I'll show you what I remember.

"The cabin looks like it has a bedroom, a kitchen and a living room. It's really just a rectangle with the kitchen on the east end, the living room in the middle and a bedroom on the west end. The front door opens on the south and is pretty much in the middle. There's a back door off the kitchen that leads to a privy."

"What about vegetation and cover?" Sonny asked.

"Well, the area immediately in front of the cabin is fairly clear of vegetation, but the chaparral pretty well hides the place until you get within about twenty yards of it. There's a stand of open bull pine behind the cabin. But again, the brush makes it hard to see until you're right up to that little stand of timber."

Roger interrupted. "What's the cabin made of? Rock, lumber...?"

"It looks like it was built about fifty years ago from rough cut lumber and then just sided with that heavy felt. You know, tar paper. And it has a metal roof. You can see where the owners have cut the brush back and made some efforts to make it wildfire proof."

"But it wouldn't make a good place to fort up?"

Dale laughed, "Not unless you guys are using rubber bullets."

Bud chuckled. "Not a chance. Okay. Thanks, Dale. Any more questions?"

Patty Allison said, "I was wondering why you aren't including Jack Tipton. After all, he's the new BLM ranger."

Bud was unruffled by the question. "Because I don't know him yet. I'm sure he's a fine law enforcement officer, but we need to get a bit better acquainted."

Charlie Prince spoke up. "I don't really have a question, but it occurs to me that he could've hiked into Aspen Cabin."

"I thought about that," Sonny said. "But if he was going to Aspen Cabin, why wouldn't he take the main North Warner road?"

"I suppose you're right."

"Colonel, what've you got for us?" Bud asked.

"Here's the scoop. The state police spotter plane is going to make a pass over the cabin in about an hour. That'll be 0600. There should be enough light for them to see the cabin. They'll be looking for any sign of habitation: lights, smoke, footprints, that kind of thing. Ranger Allison and I will set up a command center here. The plane won't be on your frequency, but I will, and I'll relay anything he has to report. We have good communications with Control. Our call sign here will be Command."

"What do you have for us?" Bud asked the District Ranger.

"Here are some new copies of the GIS map. Our people ran these to show, types of vegetation, and the roads. You can see the drainage where the vehicle's stuck. And that little cabin icon is the precise location of the cabin. I see a type Four stream course to the south and east of the cabin you might find useful."

"Type Four?" Bud asked.

She grinned, "I'm sorry. Type Four is a riparian class. It means it sometimes carries a little snow melt in a generally dry channel."

"Well, good. That little channel might give us access to the cabin without exposing us to view."

"Gus? See anything we're missing."

"Well, you might take a blocking action on the east end of the dirt track that ties into the Plush highway. I don't imagine he'll take off in that direction, but it wouldn't hurt to have someone there."

"Got anybody in mind for that chore?"

"I sort of thought I'd take that. These old bones don't like running the hills as much as they used to."

"Okay. That's a good idea. Now, I want to talk safety. Our objective is to bring this guy in without anyone getting hurt. I want him healthy and able to stand trial. On the other hand, the rules of reasonable force are in effect. And I want everyone who's going with us to wear body armor. Be aware of where your partners are. And I want each of you to carry a water bottle and a first-aid kit. I'll take the big kit on my horse.

"We're going to take Breon with us until we're within about four hundred yards of the cabin. He'll guide us. There's an extra horse in the trailer for him. When we reach the drop off point, I want you, Mr. Breon, to turn around and get the hell out of there. Quietly. Okay?"

"I am a natural born coward, Mr. Blair."

"I doubt that, but I'll trust you to do as I ask just the same. Michelle and I are going to ride as close as we can get to the cabin without tipping Casey off. We'll take up position and then I want Sonny and Charlie coming up the middle, Roger and Tom coming up that little drainage. When you all have the cabin in sight, call in. I'll approach the back door while you all cover me. When I'm in place, Roger is going to make an approach from the southeast corner to the front door. When Roger reaches the front door, Michelle will give us the go signal. Hopefully, he'll still be asleep. Any questions?"

"You trying to take care of me?" Michelle asked.

"No way. You're a better shot than I am. You'll be taking care of me."

"I want one officer to carry a rifle. The rest can carry shotguns. Tom, you any good with a rifle?"

"Yes sir. I qualified expert at the range."

"Ever shoot anybody?"

"No."

"Me either. But you carry a rifle. Hopefully, you won't have to do any shooting this time. Okay. Let's head 'em up. When we get to the road, I want to unload as quietly as we can. No cussing and no slamming of doors."

The gray light of morning was just opening up the sky when they pulled off the highway and through the gate. Breon's description of a scab rock flat was accurate, but the ground was too soft to carry the vehicles, so they just pulled the trailers up the gravel road in line and started off-loading the horses. It was all nervous business now. No wisecracks, no small talk.

They led the horses up the road to the edge of a stand of short, scraggly juniper trees and waited. At almost precisely 6:20 they could hear the drone of a single engine plane. The eastern horizon was starting to pink up and the details of the hillsides were coming into focus. The plane approached the cabin from the east to take advantage of the morning light.

Bud stood beside a big bay gelding the Forest Service had loaned him for this venture. He ran the scene and the planning over in his mind, looking for anything he might have forgotten. Nothing came to mind, and then that started to work on his nerves as well. "You can't expect to remember what you forgot," he said to himself. "But there's always something." And then it popped into his mind. Gloves! He'd forgotten his gloves. Well, if that was all, they were ready to roll.

Through a gap in the junipers they could all see the plane. It just seemed to hover along, barely above stall speed. Bud held his breath and hoped it wasn't too low or too loud. The first pass probably took less than five minutes, but to Bud it seemed more like an hour. Finally, the Colonel's voice broke the silence.

"County One, this is Command."

"County One. Go ahead."

"The spotter plane reports no smoke and no lights, and no visible footprints. Either your fugitive is asleep, or he's not there."

"Got it. Thanks. I'd like another pass in about 45 minutes. I think we should be in place by then."

"You got it. Control says to approach with caution."

"Count on it. By the way, is Gus on the other end of the road?"

Gus's radio broke in. "Not quite. I'll be there in about ten or fifteen minutes."

"Well, it's a go then."

Bud turned to his officers. "Let's do it."

***

The plane hadn't disturbed William Casey's sleep. In fact, it was almost forty minutes later when he stepped out the back door of the cabin to relieve his stomach of bile and too much whiskey. It was several minutes before his dry heaves had subsided.

His head was pounding and he was still stooped over trying to rid his mouth of the last of the night before. He was in a wretched state, that much he knew. And he was in too much trouble to even think about making it right again.

It was the faint noise of the squelch breaking on a radio that alerted him. Bud cussed himself and turned his radio down. The missing link was not the gloves. It was his earpiece for the radio. For the first time in years he doubted his own capabilities as a law enforcement officer.

Casey's reaction was less than instantaneous. Senses befuddled by whiskey fumes, he wasn't really certain he had heard anything. But he went back into the house and picked up his Remington semi-automatic 30-06, pulled the slide back and let it snap shut to make sure it was loaded. Then stepped out the back door and behind a small bull-pine, watching the old road.

***

Bud was startled by the sudden appearance of the cabin as his horse stepped into the open at the edge of the mesquite. Breon was right. You couldn't see the cabin until you were right up on it. He pulled the reins to back the horse out of sight when he heard a dull whack as a bullet hit the big bay in the head, and then vaguely heard the report of the rifle that had fired the bullet.

The horse suddenly dropped and rolled over on its side. Bud was too startled by the sudden attack to pull his leg free of the stirrup; then he realized it was simply too late to do anything but lie there with his right leg pinned under the weight of the saddle and the body of the horse.

He was aware enough to get his pistol free of his holster, but he couldn't see over the bulk of the horse. Michelle bolted past him, took up a shooter's stance and emptied all fifteen rounds from her 40-caliber Glock, hit the eject button, and slammed another clip home.

Bud was shouting, "Take cover, damn it! Take cover!" And then she was out of sight. He could hear some more shooting, and then angry shouting. His leg started to throb and he knew he'd been hurt more than a wee bit.

The spotter plane droned slowly overhead not more than two hundred feet above him. Bud cussed. He knew they were going to report a disaster, and he was the chief architect of that disaster.

"County One, this is Command."

He hit the button on his lapel mic. The damned thing wouldn't send.

"County One, do you copy? We have a report of an officer down. What's going on over there?"

"I don't know. I can't see a damned thing," he shouted into his useless microphone.

"Do you have an officer down?"

"Yes, damn it. Me. My horse is lying on me and I can't move." Sonny's voice came on the air. "Command, this is County Two. It's under control here. Casey is in custody, but I don't know how bad the sheriff's hurt. I'm on my way to check him."

"County Two, do you want us to roll an ambulance?"

"Yes. Do it."

Michelle's voice broke through the fog of Bud's anger and frustration. "Bud, are you hit?"

"No, damn it," he gritted out. "This damned horse is trying to crush me. I think Casey shot the poor beast out from under me. No, correction…on top of me. And my damned radio quit working. Is anyone else hurt?"

"We're all okay, Bud."

His run from the cabin and his anxiety had Sonny panting. He peered anxiously over the belly of the horse. "Are you hurt?"

"I'm beginning to think so. Could be this nice horse has broken something. I landed on my pistol. And there's a boulder about the size of a boxcar under my ankle. What about Casey?"

Michelle's eyes grew angry. "That stupid, stupid son-of-a-bitch shot your horse and then shot at me, and I couldn't hit him. When he ran out of ammo, Roger tackled him. Casey took a swing at

Roger, so Tom clipped him alongside the jaw with the butt of his rifle. He's out cold."

Sonny looked at her and then started to chuckle. "Oh, you didn't exactly miss him. You hit the tree he was standing behind six times. Right at the level of his inhuman heart."

"I did?"

"Yep."

"Damn it, you two. Let's do a postmortem later," Bud said through gritted teeth. "Get some help over here and see if you can roll this poor beast off my leg."

Sonny hollered, "Hey you guys, get over here. The sheriff's had a slight mishap. We need to get this horse off him."

"County Two, this is Command."

"County Two."

"The ambulance is rolling. How's Bud?"

"Can't tell for sure. He doesn't appear to have internal injuries, but there's a good chance his leg is broken. We won't know until we get his horse off him. He's cracking jokes, but he's hurting some. And I think he's starting to go into shock."

"Copy. I'll let the ambulance know. Command clear."

Roger located a small log near the woodpile behind the cabin while Charlie and Tom searched the cabin and found a stout piece of rope about twenty feet long. Then they tied the rope from the saddle horn on Tom's horse to the saddle horn on the uphill side of Bud's dead horse. Roger said, "Okay, I'm going to slide this pole under the horse near Bud's leg. When I give the word, Tom you take up as much slack as you can with your horse and Charlie and I'll lift as much as we can. Michelle, you and Sonny drag Bud loose. Ready? On three. One, two, three...heave!"

The twelve-hundred-pound horse on Bud's leg rolled up slightly and Michelle and Sonny pulled Bud loose just before the pole broke. Roger and Charlie went sprawling sideways and Tom's horse staggered backwards. But Bud was free and groaning through clinched teeth. Roger got up and dusted himself off. "Well, there goes my bonus money."

Bud grinned in spite of himself. "You paying for this dead animal?"

"No, just figured it wasn't too smart to hurt the boss."

Bud glanced up at Charlie. "I'm damned glad you were here. Ol' Roger is pretty stout, but I don't think even Roger could bust a six-inch log."

"He could bust this one. It was a tad rotten."

The radio interrupted their not-so-clever repartee. "County Two. Command."

"Go ahead."

"Believe it or not, the ambulance just rolled past us. It should be at the turnoff in about four or five minutes. Breon is ready and waiting to bring in a litter."

"Any medical advice?"

"If you use channel nine, you should be able to raise the EMTs in the ambulance now."

"Copy."

Bud said, "I don't need any medical advice, but I could use a spot of water and a couple of aspirin."

Michelle was cussing the dead horse. "He fell on the big first-aid kit."

"Well, we'll just cut the cinch and use my horse to drag the saddle loose. In the meantime, see what the blood on Bud's right arm is all about," Tom ordered.

Roger rolled his jacket to make a pillow for Bud, and Michelle covered him with hers. "No aspirin until we hear from the EMTs," she said. "You're tough."

"How about some water, then. Or whiskey."

Tom cut the saddle cinch, mounted his horse and guided it forward. There was a temporary strain on the rope, and then the saddle slipped from Bud's horse. Michelle began tearing into the first-aid kit.

Roger started squeezing Bud's right leg, working from the hip slowly toward the ankle. When he touched the bone just above the ankle, Bud winced.

"That hurt?"

"Damned right, it hurts. But not as much as my knee and my hip. When we get through this, you're all going to take some refresher training in the first-aid business."

Sonny tried channel nine. "Lakeview ambulance, this is Deputy Sixkiller. How do you read?"

A male voice with a slight western drawl said, "Five by five. Go ahead."

"The sheriff seems to have a broken ankle and other injuries to his hip and knee. He may have a broken elbow as well." He watched Roger and Michelle fit the inflatable splint on Bud's leg and start blowing it up. "We have a splint on the leg, but he'll have to be littered out. Can you ride a horse?"

"I like the gentle ones best, but I do ride rodeo on weekends."

"Is that Justin Marks I hear?"

"Yep, one and the same."

"Okay, we'll have a horse for you, Justin. I don't want to move the sheriff until you get here. How about giving him some Tylenol?"

"Negative. Just keep him warm and give him non-alcoholic liquids until I can examine him. Any place in there big enough for a helicopter?"

"Not a chance. The only clearing that big is by our rigs next to the highway."

"Okay. We'll get to you as soon as we can."

"Sixkiller clear."

***

EMT Justin Marks, his lean figure keeping perfect rhythm with his loping horse came up the old road to the cabin. Breon followed, dangling a litter alongside his mount.

Bud was in a half-daze, and slightly puzzled by all the fuss. He could move his arm, but the leg was simply killing him. Especially the hip. The ankle had swollen in his boot and was causing a lot of pressure and pain.

"I need to get my boot off," he said.

Marks just grinned and said, "No, that makes a pretty good cast." He took Bud's pulse and checked his blood pressure and then started an IV. He then cut the sleeve of Bud's new down jacket up beyond the elbow. Bud grumbled about ruining a perfectly good jacket. The elbow was swollen, and there was a deep puncture that was bleeding slightly, but the elbow didn't appear to be broken. Justin carefully positioned Bud's right arm across his chest and taped it in place. With Marks coaching them, Bud's officers lifted and placed him on the litter. Without preamble or discussion, Roger took one end of the stretcher and Charlie the other.

The trip to the ambulance was an agony for Bud. A rancher who had been listening on his base radio to the police band, loaded up his off-highway vehicle, a 4x4 Goat, and headed to the scene with his son. He was putt-putting up the cabin road when the sweating stretcher bearers reached the snowbank and Casey's stranded Ford pickup.

They lashed Bud's litter on the rear deck of the goat, and then jounced and bounced the three quarters of a mile down the rutted, rocky road to the highway and the ambulance while Jimmy Higgins, the rancher's son, cracked jokes about freeway traffic and horse chestnuts.

Bud saw Roger putting Casey in the back of Trooper Prince's cruiser. Then Marks closed the ambulance doors and the driver eased out on the highway and sped west back towards Lakeview. When the driver hit the siren, Bud laughed and groaned.

"What's the hurry? I'm bunged up, but I'm not going to die."

"You let us do our job, Sheriff. Just lie back and enjoy the ride."

Nancy Sixkiller was waiting at the emergency room doorway when the ambulance pulled in. As the EMTs unloaded the gurney, popped the legs down and started through the doorway, Nancy walked beside him, patting his arm.

"You all right?"

"Of course. What else? I just screwed up big time. That's all."

"Where are you hurt?"

"Ankle, knee, hip, elbow. Pride."

The ER nurse shooed Nancy away, and then whisked Bud's gurney behind a pullback curtain, which she closed behind her. Dr. Kohl came hurrying into the ER.

Two hours later Bud was propped up in bed, staring remorsefully at the brand-new cast that ran from ankle to mid-thigh.

When Nancy walked into the recovery room, he was still floating from some sort of pain medication. He'd tried to resist, but Dr. Kohl administered it anyway via a big, long, ugly, vicious needle. Bud hated needles. He wouldn't even let the dentist give him Novocain.

"Hello, Bud. How you feeling?"

He stared intently at her for a minute. "Are those tears I see?"

"The radio scared me to death. When I heard the spotter plane calling 'officer down,' I knew it was you, and I knew you were dead, and I knew I couldn't stand the thought. And then when they said you were hurt, but you would live, I was angry. What were you doing out there, running around in the brush like a…like a damned commando?"

The long day, the injuries, and the pain medication caught up with him all at once. His eyes closed, a faint smile on his lips, he muttered, "Gorgeous, just gorgeous."

***

By suppertime, visitors started drifting in, and his father had phoned to check on him. Bud reassured his dad that he was all right. "No, Dad, I'll be just fine. And I have lots of help. Why don't you save your visit for next summer?"

He was awake again when Asa Connor stopped by. Bud asked, "What day of the week is it?"

"It's Saturday."

"Good Lord. It's sure been a busy four days, hasn't it?"

"I know. What ever happened to sleepy Lake County? You know, Bud, I sometimes wonder if you don't bring business with you." And then he laughed.

The next morning, Dr. Kohl took the sling off Bud's arm and told him the elbow was not fractured. He also said Bud was lucky he didn't have to have ankle surgery, then gave Bud forceful admonitions about taking it easy, staying off the leg as much as possible, keeping it propped up, and coming back next Friday for another set of x-rays... Half-listening, Bud just nodded, saying, "Yes, sir, I will."

Nancy was waiting to take him to his house on the highway north of town when he was released. Sonny and Michelle and Roger wanted that duty for themselves, but when they saw the determined set of Nancy's jaw, they backed down. After what was almost a confrontation with Nancy, Michelle said to Sonny, "I think your sister has made up her mind. I wonder if Bud has figured that out yet?"

Sonny roared with laughter until tears coursed down his cheeks.

"Comic relief?" Michelle asked.

"Maybe, but I had this flashback to our childhood when Nancy and I were growing up. She was the most stubborn, the most determined human being west of the Mississippi. Even when we were just playing games, if she decided the game was going to be played a certain way, we did it her way. Always. One time, we were playing Monopoly, I think I was about six and she was about nine, and she didn't want me to buy a certain property, and when I bought it anyway, she just tossed the board and all the pieces up in the air and stomped off."

Michelle grinned. "I have a brother like that, but he's just a sore loser."

Sonny looked at her. "Yeah, that too."

***

Molly was barking from the backyard when Nancy pulled off the highway and into Bud's driveway. "I fed her last night," Nancy said. "Thanks. I guess I forgot about her there for a few hours."

Nancy came around to the passenger side of her Toyota pickup and helped Bud slide to the ground. His jaw was clamped shut, and he grunted a little when he was finally standing on the ground. Nancy helped him get a crutch under each arm and held open the back gate while he grimaced and gingerly tested his one-leg-two-crutch swing.

At the back door, he put the crutches in one hand and tried standing on one leg, fumbling with the screen door. Nancy put her arm around his waist, held the screen open, and helped him hop into the kitchen.

He put his arm around her shoulders. It felt surprisingly normal and intensely personal. A faint whisper of perfume stirred old, old memories, and on a sudden impulse he squeezed her shoulder and damn near kissed the top of her head. She looked suddenly up into his hazel eyes and hugged him back.

She settled him into his recliner in the small living room, put the TV remote on the side table, turned on his reading lamp, stacked his newspaper and his mail on his lap, and said, "Enjoy. I'll make some coffee and fix you something to eat. By the way, I called your dad. He said he thinks he picked up a flu bug, so he'll come down later.

"He said something else I found interesting. Said it was the second time you'd been shot…or shot at?" She looked at him speculatively, waiting. Finally, "Is that true?"

He looked up at her, noted her concern, shrugged. "I don't talk about it."

"Well, I want to hear it."

He took a deep breath and said, "Both times, it went bad because I screwed up." She just folded her arms and waited.

He sighed, hesitated, and then started in. "Okay, the short version. A kid was robbing a convenience store. I worked in Portland then. My partner BB and I were close by, so we answered the call. The kid had a gun, but I thought I could talk him down. Hell, he was only fifteen. But he shot me in the chest. My body armor protected me, but the slug hit me hard enough to crack my sternum and put me down. When I came to, I was in an ambulance and the kid was dead. I kept thinking that if I'd drawn my pistol first, we might've bluffed him into giving up. But, no, I had to be a hero. So the kid dies."

"And yesterday?"

"Missed me."

She didn't say anything, just looked at his craggy face, the crooked nose, and then stared into his hazel eyes. Finally, she shrugged. "Maybe. But don't you go to doubting yourself. You are very, very good at what you do. And I ..."

"And I what?"

"Never mind. I'll get some food on."

He watched her walk through the kitchen door, speculating about what she might have been going to say, hoping he was right, because maybe he was feeling the same.

He reached for his mail: a couple of offers for great deals on new credit cards, a chance to win millions of dollars, and a car insurance bill. He put the bill on his side table, tossed the rest in a handy wastebasket, and reached for the remote.

Bud had a self-indulgent side, not atypical of bachelors, and he had a very nice entertainment center, complete with good speakers, CD changer, tape deck, VCR, DVD, and TV. He punched a power button, hit "1", and sat back. A Dave Brubeck CD slid in place and "Take Five" filled the room with its syncopated rhythm.

He heard Nancy making a domestic clatter in the kitchen— water running, refrigerator door opening and closing, the drip coffee pot gurgling spasmodically, cupboard doors opening. Good, peaceful sounds. Pain or no pain, he experienced a feeling of contentment.

Nancy appeared in the doorway. "Bud, you don't have anything to eat here."

"Try the freezer on the back porch. There should be a ton of frozen dinners in there. I like the Mexican dinners. And I like them cooked in the oven, not the microwave."

"And I suppose you think I'm going to spend that much time here?"

"No, I was just stating a preference."

"Okay. Just this one time, I'll indulge you."

She brought him a hot cup of fresh coffee, set it on his side table, and then sat cross-legged on the floor in front of him, her eyes serious. "Okay, what happened?"

He looked into her green eyes, took a deep breath, sighed, and then spoke. "The bald truth is that I forgot the earpiece to my personal portable and then compounded that by forgetting to turn the volume down. When Roger and Tom were in place, they called in. I think Casey heard the call and was waiting. And then I just rode right up on the cabin before I knew it was there.

My horse and I just rode around the corner of the road, and Bang! Down he went. So much for stealth and surprise."

"You could've been killed."

"Maybe, but I had on my vest. And if Casey had aimed a little higher, the slug would probably have just punched me off the horse."

"That's not a comforting thought."

"No, but it didn't happen, and I'm still alive in my own living room talking with a beautiful woman."

She gave him an appraising glance. "Thank you. You save that for when you're healed up. I'd better go check the timer."

She came back into the living room a few minutes later with his dinner, a bottle of green taco sauce, and a pain pill.

"You know what they are calling Michelle now?"

"Nope. Haven't heard a thing."

"It's a toss-up between Trigger True Shot and Calamity Jane."

"Why is that?"

"I guess you haven't heard. She emptied a fifteen-round clip at Casey and hit the tree he was hiding behind six times, all right at chest level."

"Ouch. I could see her shooting from where I was, but the horse blocked the rest. Frankly, her shooting impresses me, but she should've taken cover. I'll have to talk to her about that."

"Listen, you pompous ass, she was protecting you."

"Ouch again."

Nancy stared hard at him, quiet for a period of about fifteen seconds. "I think you just got my dander up, Mr. Sheriff. I'm going home. I'll leave you my Toyota. It has an automatic transmission, and I know anybody as dumb as you will try to go to work tomorrow. Where's the key to your pickup? I'll drive that until you heal up."

"It was still a dumb stunt."

"You just can't see it, can you? Your officers care about you and about each other. Be grateful and shut up."

"Let Molly in on your way out."

"You are welcome," she tossed back at him as she stomped out the back door and let it slam shut.

***

True to Nancy's prediction, Bud hobbled into the office about 8:30 Monday morning. Karen looked concerned, but smiled and said, "Good morning, Gimpy." Michelle was busy at the terminal pounding out her report about the Casey arrest. She looked up when he stumbled through the door.

"Do you think that's a good idea?" she asked.

"Actually, no. My ankle's really talking to me. It keeps pace with my heartbeat. Keeps saying things like dumb, dumb, dumb. I thought I could tough it out, but just getting across the sidewalk convinced me this isn't a good idea. But since I'm here, what's going on?"

He used his good arm to turn a chair, then leaned the crutches against the wall and plopped down with his cast stiffly out in front. He tried to use his good leg to push a chair in front of the cast, fumbling and finally tipping over the would-be footstool. Michelle got up, set it in front of him, and helped him lift the cast onto the wooden visitor's chair.

"Sonny and Roger are getting a statement from Casey. I guess he cried and spilled his guts all the way to town. Charlie kept telling him to keep quiet until he had talked to an attorney, but Casey just kept babbling about not meaning to kill Gordon Gooding. About not meaning to shoot at you. Charlie said he cried and talked non-stop all the way to town. One thing of interest to Charlie was Casey's story about a big development coming into the valley, and how he wouldn't be part of it now, missed chances, life screwed up. That sort of thing."

Bud grabbed the crutches, heaved himself upright and hobbled to his office. "Come on in here."

"Deputy Trivoli, please close the door. I have something to say. About yesterday. I'm embarrassed about the whole situation. I endangered your life because I was careless. You reacted..." he paused, searching for the right words, "... splendidly, heroically, calmly. Hell, I don't know how to say it. And you were stupid as hell. Next time we get into a scrape you damned well better take some cover. That said, if I wasn't feeling so damned old and bunged up, I'd give you a hug." His eyes started tearing up. "Shit. It must be the pain medication."

She got up from her chair, went over to him and squeezed his shoulders. Her eyes were sympathetic. And then they turned hard and flat. "Bud, I thought that son-of-a-bitch had shot you, and I was damned well determined he wouldn't shoot you again. And I would've shot him if it hadn't been for the damned pine tree."

The fierce finality of her statement shocked him a bit. He just stared at her eyes.

She caught the look. "I'm not blood-thirsty, Bud."

"I know you're not," he finally replied, not entirely convinced but wanting to be. "Nancy explained it to me." He paused again, long enough to make Michelle uncomfortable. Finally, he said, "Thank you. But if there ever is a next time, please take cover. I don't want any of my officers getting hurt either."

Blessedly, the phone rang, breaking the tension. Bud didn't want to doubt any of his officers. On the face of it, Michelle had behaved extremely well, but there was something there, something he couldn't quite fathom that made him uneasy.

Michelle answered the phone, and then said, "It's for you. Sheriff Don Smith from Baker County is calling."

Grateful for the interruption, Bud picked up his phone. "Hello, you old rattlesnake. How's business?" Bud listened for a minute and then chuckled. "Well, I've been better. But thanks to Deputy Trivoli, I'm better than I might have been."

Michelle threw him a grateful glance.

"You're gonna do what? Boy, you are a glutton for punishment. Thanks. I'll give you a hand as soon as I can. I really wasn't looking forward to putting that conference together. How's Candice? You know, Candice, your wife. I'm still going to take her away from you one of these days if you don't start treating her nice."

Bud chuckled again. "Or probably not. Look, let's go catch some trout or bass one of these days, and let the young, eager beavers chase the bad guys. Okay? Thanks for checking in. Yeah, I will. You too."

He hung up. Smiled at Michelle. "You'll have to forgive an old peace officer. Want to know the truth?"

She nodded.

"I've never fired my weapon except at the range. I still don't know how I'd react if I was in your boots."

"Boss, you did just fine. Do you remember drawing your pistol? That was instinct and training taking over. That's all that happened to me."

He sighed. "Well, I'm going to type up my after-action report. And then I think I'll head back to the house. Maybe Molly and I'll go to the cabin tonight. I'll call Sonny and let him know."

He was just printing a copy of his report when Howard Finch came bustling into the office.

"Hey, Bud. How you doing? Shot any horses lately?" He laughed at his own miserable humor.

"Howard, don't you go starting rumors. It's bad enough as it is."

"Not so. Your officers just brought me a signed confession, and I'll have the autopsy report by this afternoon. Not a bad couple of days' work, Bud. I'm sorry as hell about your leg, but this case is going to get me re-elected. And you too."

"Not if you ragging me about shooting my horse."

The phone rang and Michelle answered. "Lake County Sheriff's Office. Oh, hello Charlie. They did? That's wonderful. Can you fax that over? That was quick." She paused. "I don't know. The sheriff's bunged up and we're shorthanded right now. Let's just do lunch tomorrow. Okay. See you then."

Bud and Howard were listening, and Howard plumped into Sonny's chair. "Hmmm, do I sense a budding romance?"

She blushed, and Bud started laughing, and then the dam just broke. He roared with laughter until the tears streamed down his cheeks. "My, God," he finally choked out, "Saturday, she's grimly trying to shoot a man, and today she's blushing like a school girl."

"Maybe you're just suffering from a delayed reaction," she retorted with a smile, suddenly feeling better.

He wiped his tears. "No, I mean it. I'm sorry. I think you and Charlie make a fine couple. Now, what was this other news?"

"He said the lab lifted a good print from one of the .308 rounds from the truck the rustlers were using. They ran it through AFIS and they have a match. Charlie is having the lab fax a copy here." Bud looked at Howard, "How about that. Maybe we can nail this one down too. Any report back on prints from the whiskey glasses or the shards, Michelle?"

"Yes, a copy of the report is on your desk. Mr. Finch has a copy and we have the original in the file. Casey's prints were on one of the whiskey glasses, Gooding's on the other, and we have a partial match to Casey's fingerprints on the neck of the whiskey bottle."

Howard rubbed his hands in glee. "Gotcha, Casey! What about DNA?"

"The lab is waiting on the sample. I mailed that off this morning."

Bud smiled. "On that happy note, I'm going home and then out to the lake."

Bud was gone about twenty minutes when the phone rang again. Michelle answered. "This is Deputy Trivoli. Thanks. How are things in Ely? Did I say that right? It's 'Elee' not 'Eli?'" She paused and listened. "So Alfred Gooding's activities last week are accounted for. Well, that's good, and I'm not surprised. We have a man in custody who confessed to the murder.

"Do you know if Alfred Gooding is coming to Lakeview? Okay, we'll be expecting him. And thanks for the good work. If you get out this way, stop and see us."

***

Bud hobbled into his living room. The throb in his ankle convinced him a trip to the cabin was out of the question. He sat in his recliner scratching Molly's ears and waiting for a pain pill to take effect. "Molly, I think we'll have to stay home tonight. If I'm up to it, we'll go to the cabin tomorrow." Her tail thumped the carpet and she licked at his hand.

The back door swung open, and Nancy called, "Bud, you awake?"

"Come on in. I'm in the living room."

She stopped in the doorway between the kitchen and the living room, holding out two plastic grocery sacks. "I brought some food since you don't keep any here. Have you had any breakfast?"

"No, I just didn't feel like it. You still mad at me?"

Nancy ignored the question. "Well, I brought you some good coffee, a warm cinnamon roll, and some orange juice. I hope you like cinnamon rolls."

"Love 'em."

"Deputy Trivoli told me you were being stupid this morning. So I also brought the case file on Gooding, and her after-action report. Sonny and Roger are working on theirs. They'll bring them out later. And we'll run anything else you need out here, so you don't need to come into the office. How's the leg?"

"Let me see. Yes, I was being a tad stupid. The leg is going to be all right. Thanks for the coffee and the files. And no, I'm not going anywhere."

CHAPTER 10

On Tuesday, the Lake County News carried a front-page story about the arrest of William Casey for the murder of Gordon Gooding, "a native of Lake County and a long-time rancher." The article also contained a bald account of the "alleged" shooting of the sheriff's horse, Bud's subsequent injury, and a quote from Judge Lynch about the "excellent work of the Lake County Sheriff's Department, and the cooperating law enforcement agencies, the U.S. Forest Service, the Oregon State Police, and the Lakeview City Police Department."

Bud grinned when he read that. Lynch could find political leverage in a disaster.

***

In the office of the vice president of the Land and Cattleman's Bank, Franklin Pierce was also reading the article with interest. The mention of Alfred Gooding was worrisome. He picked up his phone and dialed Susan McDowell's extension. She answered, "Good morning. Land and Cattleman's Bank."

He simply said, "Tonight."

She answered, "Thank you, sir. We can do that." And then they both hung up.

***

Bud sat at his kitchen table sipping coffee from a heavy white mug, rereading the case file, and listing the evidence on a yellow legal pad. He had tried to study it the previous day, but the pain medication made him spacey and unable to concentrate. So, this morning he was going without. "And it hurts like hell," he said to Molly when he filled her food dish on the back porch.

The case seemed pretty much cut-and-dried. They had a body. They had a confession from Casey saying he had struck Gordon Gooding in the head with a whiskey bottle.

Casey's confession covered the details and the physical evidence of the incident. Bud made a list:

Casey goes to the Gooding ranch and
Takes along a bottle of whiskey
They have a drink
Casey offers to buy the ranch
Gooding goes outside to outhouse
Casey follows
They argue
Gordon Gooding hits Casey with his cane
Casey hits Gooding with the whiskey bottle
The rancher dies
Casey tries to make it look like an accident

Bud set the evidence file aside and started reading the autopsy report. It included a transcript of a tape recording:

"This is State Pathologist Steven Rodgers. Assisting me is Dr. Marion Hudson. The deceased, Gordon Gooding, is a Caucasian male, age sixty-eight. Height five feet ten inches. Weight one hundred and seventy-three. There is a small tattoo on his left shoulder, a heart with the name Mamie. There is evidence of trauma to the right side of the skull."

Bud made a note on a yellow legal pad: Is Casey right-handed or left-handed?

Bud read doggedly through the report, making notes.

Trauma to the right side of skull
Arthritic right knee
Airway blocked by mud

The third entry sent him hurrying to the end of the report. *Cause of death: asphyxiation.*

"Damn, Molly. Let's read this again." He picked up the file and started rereading Casey's confession. "Wow," he said when he had finished reading it. "We need to rethink this."

The phone rang, and he banged his cast against a table leg getting to it. He cussed under his breath before he barked, "Speak."

"You still an unfriendly son-of-a-bitch."

"BB?"

"None other. The grapevine has it some hick cowboy shot you. Is that true?"

"Did you call to offer sympathy or just to check on rumors?"

"Hey, you onto it, Honky. So what's going on? How you feeling?"

When Bud finished relating his tale and going over the case evidence, the autopsy report, and the timeline of events, he had the case firmly in his mind. BB said his get well and goodbye, and Bud dialed the station.

"Sonny? Who's in the office? Okay. I'd like you and Michelle to gather up Howard Finch and come out to the house. I need to go over the Casey file with you. I don't think Casey actually killed Gooding. I'll explain when you get here."

Bud hung up and looked at Molly. He grinned and she got up off her piece of rug by the back door and padded over to him. He patted her head, scratched her ears, and said, "Molly, old gal, I feel better than I have in several days. You want out?"

She wagged her tail and Bud almost forgot the pain as he rose, slipped a crutch under each arm, and hobbled to the door to let her into the back yard. He started a fresh pot of coffee in the drip brewer, and without being aware of it he whistled a few bars of an old song called "Heartaches."

Twenty minutes later, Howard Finch's dark blue Subaru Outback skidded to a halt in Bud's graveled driveway. Molly stood at the back gate, head up, alert. She barked, and Bud hollered, "Molly, it's okay."

Sonny's pickup and Michelle's Ford Explorer pulled in behind Howard. Bud watched through the kitchen window as Michelle turned her vehicle around and backed it in, nose pointed back at the highway.

He was sitting at his kitchen table—an old chrome legged, Formica topped "bachelor special"—when Howard came stomping up the back steps.

Howard all but tore the back door off its hinges getting into the house. His face was red and his rich baritone voice filled the kitchen. "Mr. Henry Blair, the High Sheriff of Lake County and all-around pain in the ass, tells me my cut-and-dried case against Mr. William Casey is flawed. Hell, Bud, the arraignment is this Friday. The grand jury met this morning and handed down an indictment. We're fast tracking this."

"Well, good morning to you too, Howard. Get yourself a cup of coffee and sit down. You'll still be able to prosecute Casey, but you won't be prosecuting him for murder."

Sonny and Michelle watched the exchange between the two old friends from the open doorway.

Bud waved them on in. Then he grinned. "Don't just stand there gaping. Come on in. I made fresh coffee. Help yourself and drag up a chair."

"Damn it, Bud," Howard finally said. "I was hoping for a nice, clear-cut prosecution. This'd better be good."

Michelle and Sonny filled coffee cups, took off their standard issue Lake County Sheriff's Office brown Stetsons, and leaned back on Bud's kitchen counter, watching the two friends spar.

"Howard, I feel bad about this, but our case has been nagging at me, so I went over it again. I don't want you pissed off at me. Even Casey thinks he killed Gooding. It was an easy mistake.

But there are things that don't fit. I can't see us ignoring those just to get a conviction."

"Who do you think did it then?" Finch asked, some of the anger bleeding away.

Bud ignored the question.

"Let's go through it piece-by-piece. First, think about the behavior of William Casey. He's rash and prone to quick anger, the kind of person who just lashes out without thinking of the consequences. He's not cool when trouble comes along. So ask yourselves... can you see Casey staying calm enough to move the body, stage an accident, and clean up the evidence? I can't."

"No, I can't either," Sonny said. "He'd get rattled."

"Second, there's the timing of Casey's call to Pierce. He called Pierce at three-thirty. According to Doc Loeffler, Gooding could have died as late as four."

"And how much of the whiskey bottle did we find? The broken neck of the bottle and two tiny pieces held together by the label. Which tells us someone tried to clean up the glass. Whoever it was just overlooked the broken neck of the bottle because it was over by the outhouse. And it took Sonny's sharp eyes to spot the small pieces. Right?"

Bud spread out the full-color glossies on the table. They all leaned forward to get a better look. "Sonny took these pictures from the loft. You can get a pretty good feel for the whole yard. In this one, the stake with the yellow flagging is where Sonny found Gooding's cane. Now look at this picture. You can see the indentations in the mud from the risers on the stretcher. That's almost seventy feet from the outhouse where Sonny found the old man's cane."

"And I found drag marks under the pine needles when I checked again. I just haven't taken the time to develop the pictures," Sonny added.

"So," Michelle interrupted, "if Casey was telling the truth, he and Gooding had a fight over by the outhouse, the old man hit him with his cane, and Casey smacked him with the whiskey bottle. Then Casey panicked and ran."

Howard harrumphed and then said, "So what you're telling me is that someone else came along later, moved the body and tried to make it look like Gooding had fallen out of his barn loft?"

"That's right. But there's more. I don't think that 'someone' found a dead body. I think Gooding was still alive." Bud let that hang for a few seconds. He picked up the autopsy report and opened it to the last page.

"Look at the medical examiner's conclusion. Cause of death: asphyxiation.' In a sense, Gooding drowned in the mud of his barnyard."

Finch frowned. "So, someone moved Gooding to the end of the barn and then held his face in the mud until he died?"

"Yes. That's what I'm saying. And then whoever it was made a crude attempt to make it look like a fall. If we use that theory, the mud on the stairs up to the loft makes sense."

"Yes," Michelle added. "But whoever it was overlooked the spider webs."

"Just like Bud and I did until you pointed them out," Sonny agreed. Then he added, "Casey was wearing cowboy boots when we arrested him. The soles were pretty smooth, not cleated. And the cast we made was of a lug tread of some sort."

Howard sipped his coffee and looked at them one by one. "Money."

"Okay," Bud nodded, "talk money."

"I received a copy of Gooding's bank records this morning. Three weeks ago, he deposited $35,000 in his checking account. Then he wrote a check to the county paying up all the back property taxes, and another to the Les Schwab tire store for new tires, along with some smaller checks for gas, groceries, whiskey, that kind of thing."

"And he paid Asa cash for some no trespassing signs. So where did he get the money?" Bud asked, then answered his own question.

"From someone who wanted to get their hooks into that ranch. His son? Or maybe Pierce?"

Sonny frowned, looked at Bud, and shook his head. "I think we need to talk to Casey again. I believe everything he said about the fight with Gooding. I mean, he's confessed to murder, so why would he hold anything back? There's gotta be a connection to Pierce that Casey's not talking about. It never occurred to me to ask him what he did after he went home. If he called Pierce, that would explain why Pierce was at the ranch."

Michelle chimed in, a degree of excitement in her voice, "And Pierce could've dragged the unconscious Gooding to the barnyard and staged it to look like Gooding had fallen out of the hayloft and into the mud."

"I think that's what happened," Bud said, looking pleased. "A theory as to motivation is easy. Somehow, Casey and Pierce knew about the land developers in Bend. Pierce made no effort to hide his interest in buying the ranch. What did he say in his statement to you, Michelle? He was there to make an offer on Casey's behalf to buy Gooding's ranch?"

"So," Howard said, forgetting his pout about the grand jury, "Casey sends his banker friend to see if Gooding's really dead. Only he isn't, and Pierce sees a chance to be rid of Gooding, knowing if it isn't successful, then Casey will take the rap for Gooding's murder. Right?"

"Something like that," Bud agreed. He tapped his cast. "I'm not much at running around, but I hope you agree that we have enough suspicion to subpoena Pierce's bank records. And we need a search warrant for Pierce's house. If we should be so lucky as to find a muddy boot that matches the tread marks, I think we can build a strong case."

"You know," Howard said, his voice rising in volume until the house fairly resonated to his deep baritone, "my interest in this case was primarily intellectual. It's a terrible thing to kill someone, an awful thing. And killing in anger is almost—not quite, but almost—understandable.

"But killing a person who is in a helpless state really takes the cake. If we prove that's what Franklin Pierce Junior did to Gordon Gooding, I'm going to nail his ass. We're talking first degree murder here! Premeditated, cold blooded murder!"

"Easy, Howard. Don't pop a gasket," Bud said. "But I do like to see fervor in our public servants. I'm sorry about the grand jury. We just stopped short in our investigation because we thought we had the right person in custody."

"You're forgiven. I'd have done the same thing.

"A visit to the Land and Cattleman's Bank is in order." Howard looked at the deputies. "Shake Pierce up, but do it legally. I don't read him to be a strong character, so he might fold if you pressure him. Your boss and I are going have another chat with Casey."

Sonny and Michelle put their coffee cups on the counter, picked up their brown Stetsons and started for the door. "We're on it."

***

Wearing the orange jumpsuit with "Prisoner" stenciled on the back, Casey sat at a battered interview table looking nervously at the one-way glass. Dark circles sagged under his bloodshot blue eyes, and a large bruise ran along the left side of his jaw.

Bud studied him through the one-way glass. *He looks like he was rode hard and put away wet.*

***

"Sit," Howard said to Bud. "His attorney will be here in a minute."

"No. It's easier on my leg to lean against the wall."

"What's this about?" Randolph Emerson Elkins snapped at Howard as he hurried into the booking room.

"We have a couple of questions for your client. We want to know what he did after he got home from killing Gordon Gooding."

"Allegedly," Elkins corrected.

"All right, allegedly," Howard conceded.

"How is that germane to the charges you're bringing against my client?"

Howard glanced at Bud, shrugged, and said. "Well, as strange as it may seem, it's possible, just possible that while your client is sincere in his belief that he killed Gordon Gooding, someone else actually committed the murder."

"And we think he may know who that someone is," Bud added.

Randolph Emerson Elkins raised his eyebrows, shifted his briefcase to his right hand, stroked his chin with his left, and finally said, "And?"

Howard grimaced. "New evidence seems to indicate..." He glanced at Bud, who nodded. "Seems to indicate the deceased wasn't dead when Casey left him."

"What evidence?"

"I don't want to share that until we ask your client a couple of questions."

Elkins rubbed his chin again, thoughtful. "Okay, but if he answers the questions and it's clear that this 'mystery' person is a likely suspect, I want the charges against my client dropped."

"Only the murder charge. I'm still going to charge him with aggravated assault, attempted murder, and felonious destruction of public property—that is the death of a government horse."

"Deal," Casey's attorney said. "Let's talk to him."

Karen Highsmith, in her role as bailiff, pushed the buzzer and let them all into the interview room.

Elkins sat in a chair next to his client, and Finch took a chair across the table from them both. Bud leaned against the wall trying to ease the pressure on his throbbing ankle and wondered if it had been smart to skip the pain medication.

Elkins said to his client, "This is Howard Finch, our district attorney, and I believe you know the sheriff."

Casey was slumped over, staring at the table, not looking up. "Mr. Finch and the sheriff would like to ask you a few more questions. You don't have to answer them, but I think it would help your situation if you did."

Casey finally looked up, a questioning wary glance in his eyes. "Okay."

Howard placed a small tape recorder on the table, turned it on, and said, "This is Howard Finch, District Attorney for Lake County, Oregon. The date is Tuesday, April 18, 2000. The time is 9:50 a.m. Present are Randolph Elkins, attorney for William Casey, William Casey, and Lake County Sheriff Henry Blair.

"Mr. Casey, do you consent to this interview?" Elkins nodded, and Casey said, "Yes."

"Do you have any objections to having this interview tape recorded?"

Elkins shook his head, and Casey said, "No."

"Let the record show that Mr. William Casey, in the presence of his attorney, has consented to having this interview taped."

Howard nodded at Bud. Bud asked, "After the fight with Mr. Gordon Gooding, where was Gooding lying?"

"He was under a pine tree next to the outhouse."

"Was he lying face up or face down?"

"He was on his back."

"Did you strike him with a whiskey bottle?"

"Yeah, but only after he hit me with his cane. I can show you the bruise on my leg where he whacked me."

"So, he hit you and you hit him back?"

"Yeah."

"What were you fighting about?"

"Well, hell, he wasn't working his ranch, and I talked to Frank—that's Franklin Pierce, the banker—about borrowing money to buy Goody's ranch. So I took a bottle of Jack Daniels over to sort of soften him up. But that old son-of-a-bitch wouldn't even talk about it."

"Had you been drinking?"

"Yeah, I guess I had."

"When you struck him with the whiskey bottle, did it break?"

"It just shattered. There was glass all over the place."

"Did you think you had killed him?"

"I don't know. I thought I might have. He was just lying there so still that…I don't know…he looked dead."

"What did you do then?"

"Hell, I jumped into my pickup and tore out of there."

"Where did you go?"

"I went home."

"What did you do then?"

Casey hesitated and looked at Elkins. Elkins nodded. "I called Frank."

"Why didn't you call 911?"

"I don't know. I was scared."

"What did you tell Mr. Pierce?"

"I told him I thought I'd killed Goody. I wanted him to go check on him, help him maybe if he wasn't dead. Hell, I don't know."

"Did Mr. Pierce call back?"

"Yeah, he called on his cell phone. He said Goody was dead, but he'd take care of it. Not to worry. He'd make it look like an accident."

Howard raised his eyebrows at that, leaned forward and pushed the tape recorder a bit closer to Casey. "You're sure that's what he said? 'He'd make it look like an accident?'"

"Yeah. That's what he said. It would look like an accident, like he fell out of the barn. Goody, I mean."

"What did you do then?" Bud asked.

"Well, I was really shook up, so I had a drink. And then I guess I just panicked, so I loaded up my camping gear and headed for that old cabin. I needed some time to think."

Bud cleared his throat and asked, "Are you right-handed or left handed?"

Casey looked puzzled, glanced at Elkins who nodded. "I'm left-handed. What's that got to do with anything?"

Bud decided to push it. "Did you beat your wife before you left?"

Elkins interrupted. "I advise my client not to answer that question."

Howard spoke into the tape recorder. "End of interview. Time 1015." He clicked it off.

"Thank you, Mr. Casey. Mr. Elkins."

Elkins stroked his chin, looked at Howard and at the sheriff. "About the charge of murder."

"Your client's testimony supports the new evidence. I'll drop the charge of murder."

Casey's face reflected pure astonishment. His jaw gaped and he stared at his attorney.

"That's all I'm prepared to discuss at this time," Howard said.

Outside on the sidewalk, Bud stood stiff-legged, leaning on his crutches. He wanted to get home and get his leg elevated, maybe take a pain pill after all. He listened impatiently while Howard lectured him about the ethics of attorney-to-attorney agreements.

"Howard," he said somewhat tiredly, "I know I pushed it a bit, but I didn't have an agreement with Elkins not to ask about the beating. Call it impulse. Call it anything you want. I just saw a chance to wrap that one up, too."

"What's with the business of left-handed or right-handed?"

"Just a loose end. If Gooding was facing his attacker, and that's a good bet given his surly nature, then the attacker was probably left-handed."

"Because Gooding was struck on the right side of his head. I don't know if I'll use that, but we'll note it for the file. Okay, okay. Let it go. Let me help you into your vehicle. Go home. Relax. It was a good interview. Now we wait and see what luck Sonny and Michelle have with Pierce. I'll go get us a warrant to search his house. And I think we should arrest him, now."

"I wonder," Bud said. "He's not a flight risk, at least not until we try to arrest him. What if we let him stew for another twenty-four hours? We might squeeze a confession out of him. I'll tell Sonny and Michelle about the content of the phone call between Casey and Pierce." He settled in the front seat of Nancy's Toyota pickup and pulled his cell phone from his coat pocket.

Howard stared at Bud and then nodded. "I'm not sure I like it, but I'll wait twenty-four hours."

***

Susan McDowell saw the two deputies first as they pushed through the big glass door into the bank. She knew who they were, even though they had their personal accounts at the other bank in town. It was habit with her. You have to study the opposition.

They came to her window. "We'd like to see Mr. Pierce, please," Sonny stated.

"He's busy right now. Can I tell him what it's about?"

"No," Sonny said quietly. "And I don't care if he's busy. You unlock that door back there, or I'll come back with a warrant, and then you'll unlock it or we'll break it down. We want to see Pierce, and we want to see him now."

She pushed a buzzer under her counter, and there was an audible click as the lock opened. The lock was something she had suggested after they decided seeing each other anyplace else in town was out of the question. Remodeling the bathroom to include a shower and adding the couch to the furniture in his office had also been her idea.

Michelle held the door for Sonny, and then it closed behind them. There was a short passage and another door. This one was a heavy wooden mahogany door with a highly polished finish.

Without knocking, they opened the door and walked in. Pierce was sitting behind his desk talking on the phone when they entered. He said a quick "Thanks" and placed the handset back in the cradle.

Pierce's gold-rimmed glasses reflected light from the heavy chandelier as he looked up. It made it difficult to read his eyes. Michelle wondered if he was aware of the effect, if it was deliberate.

Sonny walked to the front edge of the desk and leaned over, towering over the diminutive banker. "Mr. Pierce, there are a few things we would like to go over with you. Would you mind coming down to the station with us?"

"What's wrong? I gave Deputy Trivoli my statement. Am I under arrest or something?"

"Should you be under arrest?" Michelle asked, approaching the desk to stand beside Sonny, trying her beautiful best to look menacing. Sonny suppressed a grin. She sounded like a budding thespian who didn't have her lines down yet.

"No, of course not," Pierce said a bit too quickly. He was intimidated by her. After all, she was carrying a pistol and wearing a badge. And she was a woman. Women had been browbeating and intimidating him all his life.

Sonny's cell phone rang. "This is Deputy Sixkiller. Okay, Sheriff. Yes. We're in Mr. Pierce's office right now." He paused, listening. "After the fight, right? It fits, doesn't it," he stated, staring hard at Franklin Pierce. "Thanks." Sonny snapped the phone shut and turned to Pierce.

"Mr. Pierce, we have a statement from Casey that he called you after telling you he thought he'd killed Gooding. Your statement fails to mention that."

"Does it? I thought I told you he asked me to negotiate with Gooding for the purchase of the ranch."

"You did," Michelle answered, "But you failed to mention that Gooding was alive when you got there."

"He wasn't. It was just like I told you. He was lying in the barnyard, face down in the mud. It looked to me like he'd fallen from the barn loft. I called 911 and waited for the ambulance."

"No," Sonny said. "You called William Casey back, told him he had indeed killed Gooding, but not to worry, you'd make it look like an accident. Then you dragged an alive but unconscious Gooding to the barnyard, rolled him over and held him face down until he suffocated. That's how it really happened, didn't it, Frank?"

Pierce turned ashen. Sweat popped out on his forehead and his hand trembled as he reached for the phone. "I'm not answering any more questions until I talk to my lawyer. Am I under arrest?"

"Not at this time, but we want you and your attorney at the station at eight o'clock tomorrow morning. You might want to bring along a toothbrush," Sonny added.

Pierce had the handset to his ear when they turned to walk out. Sonny stopped to give him a long, tight-lipped stare and then closed the door.

Susan McDowell was more disturbed by Michelle's nervous giggle than Sonny's scowl as they walked the length of the bank and out the front door.

She tried Franklin's extension, but it was busy. Damn, what the hell is going on?

***

When Sonny and Michelle were down the block and out of sight, they stopped and Sonny started laughing. "Wow! You've got to work on your menacing."

"I think he was intimidated," she said. "Besides, from what I hear, his mama's been cowing him since he was born. I hear she's still president of the bank and Franklin is just the vice president."

"If he was scared, it's because your reputation as Trigger True Shot proceeds you."

"Not nice, Sonny. Okay, mister know-it-all, how should I act?"

"Well," he started in. "The first thing is the hat. Westerners read the hat."

"Read the hat? What in the hell does that mean?"

"Okay, let me show you," and he started walking off. "Now, if my hat is sitting high on my head, sort of tipped back like this, it means I'm taking it easy, I'm relaxed, I don't have an attitude. But if it's tipped down low to sort of shade or hide my eyes, it means don't mess with me. Of course, it could mean I'm about to take a nap." Then he laughed. "But seriously, if you watch, you can learn a lot about a person's attitude by the tilt of his hat."

"I don't believe a word of it. You just made that up."

"Nope, it's true. You ask the sheriff. He'll tell you the same thing."

"You know what I wish? I wish I could have a day off." Sonny stopped and looked at the dark circles under her eyes.

"Yep," he said, "I don't want to be insulting, but you do look like something the cat drug in. I need you here at 0800 tomorrow, so the best I can do is the rest of the day. Deal?"

"You bet. I'm going home, I'm going to feed my cat, take a nice long shower, and then sleep for a few days."

"See you tomorrow then. And Michelle, thanks for taking care of Bud out there. I know I haven't said anything, but you were great."

"Bud thinks I'm blood-thirsty."

"No he doesn't. What did he say?"

"He said 'Thanks,' and then gave me a long hard stare like he was trying to decide something."

"Don't work too hard on it. Bud likes you."

"Oh, bullshit. He likes Nancy."

"No. He likes some female attention, but in three years he's never made a pass at her. I'm thinking he likes you, but the job gets in the way."

"Enough," she said. "I'm tired and I wanna go home."

A stocky man in his mid-thirties was smoking a cigarette and pacing back and forth on the walk when Sonny got back to the station. He stopped Sonny. "I'm Alfred Gooding. Gordon Gooding is…was…my dad. Can you tell me what's going on? The Ely police asked me all kinds of questions, and then they came back to tell me he was dead. And then I got a call from an attorney here in town. He said I needed to deal with Dad's estate, make funeral arrangements, that kind of stuff."

Sonny removed his hat, held out his hand. "I hate what happened to your dad. Come on in the station. I'll catch you up."

When Sonny finished his narrative, including the belief by the district attorney and the sheriff's department that Gordon Gooding was murdered, Al Gooding just shook his head. "You know, I haven't been back since I joined the Navy. Dad and I swapped a couple of letters, and I used to call once in a while until he quit paying his phone bill and they shut him off.

"Dad spent most of his time maintaining an alcoholic glow. You know, he wasn't mean to me, but after Mom was killed in a car accident...I was fourteen...he was never the same after that. He crawled off into a bottle and just sort of stopped paying attention to anything I did, and I guess I got mad at him for that. Damn it, he lost a wife, but I lost a mother and a father all at the same time."

He stopped, embarrassed by the personal revelations. "Well, I didn't know how much I missed this place until I drove past the ranch and into town. The house looks like hell, and the fields are a mess, but damn...it looked like home. I just wanted to cry."

"So, what are you going to do?"

"I'm not sure. I'm going to see this attorney and find out about the ranch. Then I guess I'll get a funeral set. After that I'm going to call my wife and talk about moving back to the ranch."

"Got any plans? Dude ranch, casino?"

"Dude ranch? No. Mainly, I'm thinking it would be a good place to raise kids." He rose, shook hands again. "If Dad was murdered, I hope you catch whoever did it. He wasn't the greatest father in the world, but after I went through a nasty divorce, one I didn't want, I had a better feel for what losing Mom did to him."

***

Bud was asleep in his recliner when the phone rang. He looked at his watch. It was 3:00 p.m. A woman's voice asked for Mr. Blair. He identified himself and then realized it was a recorded message reminding him of his appointment with Dr. Kohl at nine Friday morning.

Lordy, what's it coming to? Recorded messages in a town of less three thousand people a hundred miles from the nearest city. On second thought, he dialed the number the female voice gave on the recording. The same female voice answered. "Dr. Kohl's office. Brenda speaking."

"Brenda, this is Bud Blair. What are the chances of seeing Dr. Kohl this afternoon? I want to get this big cast off and get a smaller walking cast for my ankle."

"It's only been a few days," she said, disapproval strong in her voice.

"I know, but I have work to do, and this thing is getting in the way."

"Hold on."

She was gone for a long two or three minutes, and then she was back on the phone. "Dr. Kohl said it isn't a very good idea, but if you can be here in about thirty minutes he'll see you." She sighed and might as well have said, "Damned fool."

"I'll be there. Thanks."

CHAPTER 11

Shortly after five o'clock, when the day's accounting was complete and the tellers' cash boxes were balanced and tucked away in the vault, Susan McDowell approached John North, her supervisor.

"Mr. North, I'm applying for a job in Newport, and I was hoping you would give me a good recommendation to attach to my application."

He looked surprised. "Well, I had no idea you were dissatisfied. Is it a better paying job?"

"Yes," she said. "Yes, it is. But it's not just that. I love the beach, and we're so far from the beach here that I don't see it enough."

She dropped her eyes demurely and added. "There is also the issue of finding male companions. I think I'll have better luck in a more populated area."

He looked appraisingly at her. "We'll miss you, Susan. You've been a real asset to the bank. As far as I know, you're the only teller we've ever had who gets flowers from her customers."

She smiled and said, "Some of them are just sweethearts."

"When do you need the letter?"

"Would tomorrow afternoon be too much trouble? I'm also going to ask Mr. Pierce for one."

"I'll get it done. And let me say again, we'll miss you."

"Thank you, Mr. North." She hit the door buzzer under her counter and hurried to the locked door that separated Franklin Pierce from the rest of the world.

Pierce was sitting on the new leather couch in his office, head bowed, elbows on his knees, holding a monogrammed handkerchief to his eyes, quietly crying when Susan McDowell entered. She sat down beside him, put an arm around his neck and pulled him to her breast.

"What's wrong, Mr. Pierce?"

"Oh, God!" he wailed, "I'm going to jail, I just know it." His body shook with sobs of self-pity and despair.

"It'll be okay, Mr. Pierce." She held him tighter. The warmth of her body and the faint odor of her perfume had a calming effect. When his sobs had subsided, he pulled free, wiped his eyes, and straightened his tie. He put his glasses back on.

"What happened, Mr. Pierce? What did the police want?"

"They accused me of killing Gordon Gooding. And I have to be at the sheriff's office at eight in the morning with my attorney. And Sixkiller told me to bring a toothbrush. I'm scared. I don't want to be arrested and thrown in jail. I have a reputation to uphold. What's Mama going to think?" His eyes started tearing up again.

"Get ahold of yourself," she snapped. "What did you do?"

And so, while she held him again, he told her the whole sorry story about the call from Bill Casey. How he had arranged Gooding's body to make it appear he'd fallen from the end of the barn. About holding him down in the mud until he died, about leaving the footprint on the ladder to add weight to the idea that Gooding had been in the loft, and about cleaning up the broken glass so no one would know Casey had been there.

"Why?"

He looked up at her. "For us. If I can get my hands on that ranch, I can get out of the bank and away from Mama and my bitchy wife. We can get rich, get married, live a new life."

She was shocked. "You idiot! We are getting rich! But what makes you think I'd ever want to marry you?"

"Well...I thought...I mean, after all we've done...together...I thought you loved me. I thought you wanted a life with me. You know...marriage, a home, that kind of thing."

"Whatever made you think killing someone was the way to get that?"

"I don't know! I guess I thought if the police didn't buy the idea of an accident, they'd pin it on Casey. He was the one trying to buy the ranch. I was just the financier."

She pulled him to her once again, holding his head against her breast, stroking his head. He started to speak, but she just shushed him.

Finally, she spoke. "You just need to deny having anything to do with the killing. Your story is that you were asked by Casey to negotiate the purchase of the ranch. Stick to your original story. Even if you are arrested, stick to your story. Keep them focused on Casey's confession. Insist that you were only at the ranch to help an old friend buy the Gooding place. Deny ever doing anything wrong. Always deny. Is there anything you're not telling me?"

He shook his head.

She stopped talking, continued stroking his head, feeling him relax. "Mr. Pierce, leave it to me. I'll take care of everything."

"Can you, Miss McDowell?"

"Oh, yes. I can." And then she helped him forget his problems for a while, and they consummated their partnership one last time.

***

The search of the house was upsetting to Barbara Pierce. She had no idea why the police would come to her house with a search warrant and then go directly to her bedroom. She demanded to know—over and over again, her pudgy cheeks red with indignation—why they were invading her home. "Don't you know who I am?" she shouted.

"We're just doing our jobs, ma'am." Sonny almost snickered when he heard himself, but managed to keep a straight face. Lord, I sound like Sergeant Friday on Dragnet.

Sonny had recruited Roger Hildebrand's father, Chief Augustus "Gus" Hildebrand, to assist in the search. Two reasons. First, he might need a witness; second, the Pierce home sat within the city limits.

While Gus kept Barbara Pierce at bay, Sonny searched the walk-in closet in the master bedroom and then went directly to the back porch. Standing there, caked with mud, was a pair of side-zipper boots. With growing excitement, he picked them up and examined the soles. Gotcha.

He carried the boots into the living room and showed them to Mrs. Pierce. "Are these your husband's?"

"Of course they are," she snapped. "I don't have a lover."

Sonny looked at the pudgy figure and the once pretty face. I guess you don't, he thought.

"Thank you, Mrs. Pierce," he said. "We need to take these with us."

"Why? Whatever in the world for?"

"As possible evidence in a crime, ma'am," Chief Hildebrand said.

"What crime are you talking about? What has Franklin done?"

"We can't discuss it right now, Mrs. Pierce," Sonny answered. Barbara Pierce, former high school cheerleader and one-time Queen of the Lake County Roundup, followed them to the front door. They were walking down the steps when she snarled, "It's that Susan McDowell." The outburst startled them. Sonny and Gus spun around.

"She's the one. Oh, they think they are so smart, but I know what goes on when Franklin works late. I've known for months. And all those bank conventions and meetings. I stay home and she goes to San Francisco! He's a bastard! And she's a whore!"

Her shoulders slumped, and then she slammed the door shut. "Ouch! Think she's right?" Sonny asked.

"Well, the town doesn't know about it. If it did, we'd have heard. That's just too juicy to keep quiet. 'Local banker seduces young teller, betrays wife and prestigious family.' But it could be…though why a woman would find Franklin Pierce attractive is a mystery."

"Well, he's not a bad looking guy," Sonny said. "And he's rumored to be rich."

"It's not that. He's just such a weasel. I think I'd like to talk to what's-her-name."

"McDowell," Sonny supplied. "Yeah, her too."

"Now?"

"No. How about tomorrow? While you arrest Pierce tomorrow morning, I'll take that good-looking deputy of yours to the bank and interview this McDowell."

"I think you'd better talk to Bud first."

"Why? Do you think I'm horning in on your case? Sonny, you're the undersheriff. You decide. Besides, this thing has moved within the city limits."

Sonny looked at Gus, and then laughed. "Don't give me that innocent look. It's starting to get interesting, and your nose is twitching like an old hound on a hot scent."

Gus grinned back. "No such thing. Call it professional courtesy. I'm just trying to help out my old friend Sheriff Blair while he's incapacitated. Besides, he'll want to be in on the Pierce arrest."

He made a futile effort to hitch his belt higher on his growing paunch. Then he crossed his arms and waited.

"You're an old reprobate, Gus. Okay. You get the McDowell interrogation, and you get Deputy Trivoli. I'll let Bud know you're assisting in the Pierce case." He paused. "And thanks. I actually think it's a good idea."

"Well, if there's a scandal in our fair community, it's only right the Chief of Police be the first to know. Unfortunately, it doesn't always work that way."

***

The phone was ringing when Bud stepped out of the bathtub. He hated tub baths, but he couldn't figure any other way to keep his new walking cast dry. For that matter, he hated casts too.

He limped and dripped his way to the phone on the nightstand, toweling as he went. His alarm clock read 5:44. "This had better be good," he growled.

He heard Asa Connor's cheerful voice. "My, aren't we happy in the morning. I know you're up. I drove by your place and saw a light in your kitchen."

"Why didn't you stop then?"

"I wanted to catch you in the shower and inconvenience the hell out of you."

"Well, you almost succeeded. I was in the tub. Can't shower with this damned cast on."

"Darn, another failure," Asa chuckled. "I want to talk to the sheriff," meaning he was about to assume his professional persona as editor of the Lake County News.

"Speaking."

"Unnamed sources say you intend to arrest Franklin Pierce Junior this morning and that Howard Finch is going to charge him with murder."

"Judas Priest, Asa! Where in the hell did you hear that?"

"Bud, police officers have girlfriends, wives, and mothers. I have Agness Lynch and her cronies, who have interesting and, so far, untraced connections in the community. None of which have I felt inclined to expose.

"I also know Chief Hildebrand and Deputy Sixkiller searched the Pierce abode late yesterday evening. And that was after Deputy Sixkiller and Deputy Trivoli talked to the vice president of the Land and Cattleman's Bank. And before you ask, the answer is 'No,' I did not hear any of this from Carol."

"Well, you don't know everything," Bud growled, thinking of Sonny's late evening call regarding Barbara Pierce's accusations of hanky-panky between Susan McDowell and her husband. "But you're close. What do you want?"

"I plan to have a photographer and a reporter at the station when Pierce and his attorney show up."

"Have you talked to Howard Finch?"

"He's not up yet."

Bud sighed. "Okay, yesterday Sonny and Michelle asked Pierce to accompany them to the station. He refused and Sonny accused him of the murder of Gordon Gooding. He wouldn't go with them and wanted his lawyer. Sonny told him to bring his attorney to the station at eight this morning."

"Will he do that?"

"He really doesn't have a choice. But Asa, he's only being arrested. There's a long way to go before he's even brought to trial."

"I know. 'Innocent until.' But his arrest is news and I intend to report it. Is Finch dropping the charges against Casey?"

"You'll have to talk to Howard. Look, I'm getting a chill standing here, so I'm gonna hang up and get dressed." Bud slammed the phone down.

When he was through struggling with the chore of getting his trousers on over the cast, he clumped to the back door to let Molly in. "Good morning, old gal. You hungry?"

He patted her head, and she whacked him with her tail and licked his hand while he poured dry food into her dish. He headed to the kitchen sink to wash the "dog" off his hands.

"You know, Molly. I could learn to hate small towns. You can't fart without somebody telling the whole town about it. Sometimes they tell the town about it even when you haven't farted."

He put fresh beans in the coffee grinder, listened until he was sure all the little chunks were pulverized, and then followed his morning make-the-coffee ritual.

Dressed in his best khaki uniform, he inspected his image in the bathroom mirror. Tan Stetson at a proper angle, straightened shoulders, and sucked-in paunch. Well, *that's the best I can do.*

He tried to get a look at the one shiny Wellington on his left foot, a wool sock on his right, covering the toes sticking out of the walking cast. The height of the mirror and width of the vanity just wouldn't cooperate. An unexpected vision of Michelle, his loyal deputy and fierce protector popped into his head. "Don't even think about it," he said aloud.

CHAPTER 12

Bud cussed as he pulled Nancy's Toyota pickup into the reserved parking behind the station. The street was packed with people, and a television van from the Klamath Falls TV station was parked in the street. Technicians were setting up cameras, and Bud recognized a reporter from the "Six O'clock News."

Microphone extended, she was trying to interview Howard Finch, who somehow managed to look a bit frumpy in spite of his new blue blazer and red-striped tie. Bud gimped up to them, said "Excuse us for a minute," and pulled Howard aside.

"Tell me you didn't have anything to do with this press circus. The man's accused, but he's not convicted. How in the hell do you expect him to get a fair trial in this town now?"

"No way. I didn't have a thing to do with it. And, I don't know how they got wind of this."

Asa edged up to them just in time to hear Howard's protest. "I'd give odds that Willa Cunningham spilled the beans. She's one of Agness's informants. She also has a brother who works for the K-Falls TV station."

Bud looked disgusted. "Well, I guess there's nothing to be done about it. You know that Pierce's attorney will start the trial before he's even arrested, don't you?"

Howard said, "It's standard business to tell the press your client is innocent."

"And the press," Asa entered the conversation, "that word that sounds so disgusting when you say it, was already here, Bud: Me."

"There's responsible press, that's you, Asa, and then there's that circus called television. I had enough of those bloodsuckers to last me a lifetime when I was in Portland."

A worried looking Carol Connor, notebook in hand, stepped up beside her father.

Howard looked at his watch. "Sorry, Bud, but it's almost show time."

"Who's Pierce's attorney."

Howard pointed to answer Bud's question. Randolph Emerson Elkins was striding up the street, his lanky figure erect and confident. His client, the much shorter Franklin Pierce Junior, dressed in a conservative blue pin-stripe suit with matching dark blue tie, was practically running to keep up.

Elkins strode directly to the TV cameras. The K-Falls reporter, a neatly dressed thirty-something woman with shoulder-length blond hair, asked, "Do you have a statement for our viewers?"

"Yes. I represent Mr. Pierce. He hasn't been arrested for any crime. And I can only say that even if he is arrested for some alleged crime, he is innocent of any wrongdoing. As a good and patriotic citizen, as well as a respectable businessman, he is here to cooperate with our diligent law enforcement officials in any way he can."

"Isn't he accused in the murder of Gordon Gooding?"

"As I said, he hasn't been charged with any crime. He is an honest citizen cooperating fully with law enforcement." Elkins smiled broadly for the camera. Then he pushed the smaller Pierce forward and into the police station.

The camera swung to Howard Finch. "Mr. Finch, is Mr. Pierce being charged with the murder of Gordon Gooding?"

Howard faced the camera, gave a bland smile and said, "I hope to have a statement for you later this afternoon. That's all I can say for now."

"Is Pierce being investigated for the murder of Gordon Gooding?"

"Again, I'll have a statement for you later this afternoon." He turned and bustled through the door of the police station.

Bud started to follow, but the walking cast slowed him down, and the TV reporter pushed in front of him. The crowd of onlookers pushed and jostled, packing around him to hear what he had to say.

"Sheriff," the reporter said, pushing a microphone up in his face, "isn't it true that you were injured apprehending William Casey, and that Casey has been charged with the murder of rancher Gordon Gooding?" The people in the crowd quieted to hear his answer.

Bud looked at her for split second, pulled the microphone closer, and said, "No comment."

He put his shoulders down and began pushing none too gently through the crowd. Over the noise of the crowd, he heard the reporter calling, "Sheriff! Sheriff!" but he didn't stop or turn as he bulldozed his way into the station. Two Lakeview City Police officers blocked the door behind him.

A red-faced Elkins had a rigid forefinger on Howard's chest. "I always knew you were a sneaky son-of-a-bitch. If you arrest my client after that three-ring circus out there, I'll immediately file for change of venue."

Howard pushed the hand away. "About the only person outside this room who knew he was coming into the station was you and your client. I'm wondering if you didn't arrange it yourselves. Trying for a little sympathy?"

Bud looked around the crowded room. The uninvited included Mayor Gladys McKnight, County Judge Tom Lynch, Asa, and Carol who had somehow managed to slip into the booking room. Counting Howard, Deputy Karen Highsmith, Michelle, Sonny, Bud and Gus, there were a dozen people squeezed into a room that was crowded when it held more than four.

"Hail, hail, the gang's all here," Bud growled. "We might as well have a party." He nodded and Sonny faced Pierce.

"Franklin Pierce, I am arresting you for the murder of Gordon G. Gooding. You have the right to remain silent. Anything…" Elkins interrupted him. "You don't have to go through that. His attorney is present."

Sonny looked at Elkins and continued, "…you say may be used against you in a court of law. You have the right to an attorney. If you can't afford one, an attorney will be provided by the court."

"Asa," Bud said.

"Yep. I know. It's official police business now. I'll go quietly."

"You shouldn't have been in here in the first place." But there was no heat in Bud's voice. "Watch yourself out there. Howard wants to be the first to announce the arrest."

"We'll just go quietly back to our little office and start writing a little article for our little paper."

"Don't you go getting sarcastic on me, Asa." He looked at Deputy Highsmith. "Please let this gentleman and the lady exit the premises through the side door."

Tom Lynch sidled up beside Bud. "I haven't talked to you since you escaped the eager hands of the nurses at the hospital. How's the leg?"

"Ankle, actually."

"Okay, how's the ankle?"

"Hurts."

"Well, maybe this will make you feel better. The county commission voted to fill another full-time deputy position. Congratulations." He smiled and held out his hand.

"What brings this good fortune my way?"

Lynch ran a hand through his wavy silver hair. "Bud, it finally hit us. Even though the resident population of Lake County hasn't changed much in forty years, the population in Klamath and in Deschutes County has almost quadrupled in that time. And it's crowding us into the twenty-first century after all. That includes twenty-first century crime. Who knows? From where I sit, that may be the hallmark of this century, the child of the twentieth century growing up and bringing us the fruit of that rearing."

"Don't think much of our child, do you?"

"I had a neighbor, years ago, who had three children: two beautiful daughters and a rotten son. I was sympathetic when her son was sentenced to the state pen. All she did was look at me and say, 'Two out of three ain't bad.'"

Bud smiled and held out his hand again. "Thanks, Tom. What are you going to tell the voters?"

Tom adjusted his western bolo tie and dusted some invisible lint from his coat sleeves. "I think I've just rehearsed my speech."

***

The interrogation went as expected:

Sixkiller: "Did you receive a call from William Casey on the morning of April 10?"

Elkins: "My client respectfully declines to answer that.

Sixkiller: "Did you go to the Gooding ranch on Wednesday, April 12?"

Elkins: "My client has already given you a statement to that effect."

And so it went for the better part of an hour. Bud fidgeted, trying to find some position that would ease the pressure on his ankle. At one point Pierce shielded his mouth with his left hand and whispered something to Elkins.

Bud was suddenly alert. Some alignment of the stars, some crucial information, something elusive had just come and gone in a microsecond. He knew it. It wasn't the whispering of client and attorney. Something else. Bud didn't push it. He knew how his mind worked. Sometimes he "slept on it," let his subconscious work it out. Finally, he shrugged and said to the mayor and the county judge, both glued to the scene, "Better than a TV program, isn't it?"

Without turning her gaze from the viewing window, Mayor McKnight shushed him.

He grinned and turned to leave the room. Unless something dramatic happened, which wasn't likely, Sonny and Michelle would have this wrapped up in another few minutes. He peeked out the office door. People were drifting away, individuals now instead of a crowd, off to the business of daily lives.

Turning to Chief Hildebrand, he smiled, "Thanks for the help, Gus."

"Glad to do it. Deputy Trivoli and I will interview Susan McDowell when this is over," he said, pointing through the glass at the interview room.

Bud headed on out the door.

***

The reporter and her supporting cast of technicians were across the street from the station, sipping coffee, talking among themselves. One of the technicians pointed to Bud as he hobbled down the walk to Nancy's truck.

He settled in the seat and was about to start the engine when the young reporter knocked on the driver's side window. She was alone, no microphone, no camera. He powered the window down. She leaned close to the open window. "Sheriff, you didn't know we were coming, did you?" It was more statement than question.

"No."

"I didn't think so. And you were offended."

"Public embarrassment of the accused went out of style a long, long time ago. Even in Lake County. We haven't put people in stocks in the public square for weeks now."

"Do you think that's what we do?" she asked.

"What you do is worse. At least in the town square, the humiliation is kept in the family. People pay their dues and then eventually live it down. What you do is increase the impact of that humiliation several million times. That's a lot harder to live with. My lord, woman, the man is still innocent until he's had a trial before a jury of his peers and found guilty beyond a…"

"Shadow of a doubt," she supplied.

"Reasonable doubt," he corrected. "What if this man was someone other than a leading citizen, a banker? What if he led a more ordinary life? A ranch hand, mechanic, bookkeeper, something like that? Would you still be so interested?"

"Murder is always of interest to our viewers."

"That's too damned bad. Murder is a sad, gruesome business."

She stepped back a half pace and looked at him with interest. "When this is over, would you agree to let me do a feature story on a county sheriff in a remote western county?"

"No!" he shot back. "Listen, lady, I've only met one reporter in my life that had an ounce of ethics. One."

"Maybe you've just met the other one," she said archly. "Don't count me out until you've seen my act."

"I tell you what. You finish your coverage of this case, and I'll watch your act. If I like what I see, I'll consider your proposition."

"Deal," she said and held out her small soft hand.

"No you don't," Bud started the engine in Nancy's Toyota. "You might just have a camera rolling."

She laughed. "I hadn't thought of that. Wouldn't that be an interesting twist."

***

He pulled into the Emergency Services Center parking lot. Nancy was on the phone when he hobbled in. She motioned to a chair and finished her call.

She turned her chair, looked him up and down and then said, "Well, how's the conquering hero? I hear we had quite a hullabaloo at the jail."

He nodded. "A regular three-ring circus complete with TV crews, crowds, and local big shots."

"The mayor and the judge too, I hear."

"You seem to hear everything. Did you also hear who tipped off the K-Falls TV station?"

"No. Why?"

"I'd just like to know. Who to keep away from, that's all."

"Well if I do hear, you'll be the first to know."

He held out the keys to her pickup. "I think I can drive my own now."

"Sure?"

"I'll find out."

***

Bud was sitting at his desk when Sonny and Michelle came back from questioning Pierce.

"So?"

"He never admitted anything" Sonny responded. Every time we asked a direct question, Elkins told him to be quiet. We booked him about an hour ago."

"You don't look happy, Bud." Michelle said. "Why not?"

"Because I have this feeling we missed something, something important. I just can't put my finger on it."

"We have a suspect in custody for the murder, and we have Casey in jail for some pretty serious charges," Sonny pointed out.

"I know, but the case against Pierce isn't all that strong. I'd like one solid piece of evidence the defense can't argue away or point back at Casey. And I'm afraid that media circus today may have created a certain amount of sympathy for Pierce. You know the culture of this place. He may be an asshole, but he's our asshole."

Sonny smiled. "I never thought of it that way."

"Gus and I tried talking to Susan McDowell," Michelle said. "She clammed up and refused to talk to us. Gus threatened to haul her in, and she still wouldn't talk to us. She may look like a sweet kid, but I think she's hard as nails."

He looked at the two deputies. "You both look pooped. Tell you what. Take a break. Come back tomorrow. I don't think we're going to do anyone a lot of good if we wear out. Besides, the major excitement's over for the moment."

He looked at Michelle. "What's up with Charlie Prince? I haven't seen him since the great fiasco."

"He's on detail to Medford for a few days," Michelle said in a neutral voice.

Bud raised his eyebrows at the tone. "Oh, I almost forgot. Lynch and the commissioners approved another full-time deputy."

"Not half-time?" Sonny asked. "Full-time."

"That's just great, isn't it?" Michelle said. "We have to get our sheriff hurt to get another deputy."

Sonny grinned at her. "Now, now. Don't look a gift horse..." He stopped. "That's not very funny, is it?" He picked up his Stetson. "I think I'll go check on old man Peel out in Westside. He was ailing last time I stopped, and he lives alone."

When Sonny had gone, Bud said, "That wasn't exactly what I meant by taking a break. What do you plan to do?"

"I'll just sit here and wait with you. I have some reports to catch up on. It's been busy around here these past few days. I thought you told me when you hired me that it was just a sleepy little ol' county."

Bud laughed. "You do sound sorta like a Georgia Peach. It really isn't always this busy. Trust me."

A steaming cup of black coffee slid across his desk, and he smiled a "thank you" at Karen Highsmith.

"Has Roger checked in?"

"No. Not yet."

"I guess I'd better give him a call."

The phone was answered on the first ring. "Deputy Hildebrand."

"More like Deputy Dog, you mean. Why aren't you out chasing the bad guys?"

"I have been. A state trooper and I arrested a poacher this morning. Right here in town."

"How'd you get so lucky?"

"The idiot tried to sell a fresh set of horns to a tourist at the tavern last night. Buffalo called me, and I called Fish and Game, who sent an Officer Hackmeyer down here from La Pine to assist in his apprehension."

"Was it somebody we know?"

"No, it was a druggie from La Pine. Said he was Robert Redford. Honest to God, that's what he said. And he denied poaching, said he bought the rack off some guy in a tavern in La Pine. It didn't add up.

"Hackmeyer said they would try to match the horns to one of the deer we found up on Dairy Creek. It was a nice rack of horns. Anyway, Hackmeyer loaded him up and took him to the new jail at the justice center in Bend. I hear you had some excitement in town."

"Circus is a better description." Bud filled him in on the morning's events, and then asked, "Any word from your informant about the meth lab in Christmas Valley?"

"You know, Boss, I think he's gone missing. The last time I called the ranch where he works, some woman claimed she didn't know him and that he'd never worked there. I think I'll wander up north and take a look around tomorrow morning."

"Okay, but you be careful. By the way, we're getting another deputy. How would you feel about some help in that end of the county?"

"Another deputy? That would be great."

"Well, keep us posted."

At noon, Nancy came walking in with Chinese take-out, paper plates, and plastic dinnerware.

"So, who's hungry?"

Bud's resolve to never mix his personal life with business crumbled. He realized he really, really liked Nancy Sixkiller—the way she walked, the timbre of her voice, her perfume, those deep green eyes. And he was starving.

Nancy watched with amusement as he wolfed down fried shrimp, rice, and pork chow mien. "Skipped breakfast again, didn't you?"

"Nope. I had coffee."

"So, what does your fortune cookie say?"

He broke open the vanilla cookie, held the little scrap of paper at arm's length, and then finally took his reading glasses out of his pocket. "It says, 'Either get longer arms or better glasses.'"

Michelle and Nancy both laughed. "No, I'm serious," Nancy said. "Read it."

"Hmmm. Well, it says, 'Romance and laughter to come your way.'"

Nancy made a playful grab for the scrap of paper. "Does not."

"Does too, but you can't show it to anyone, or it'll break the spell."

Michelle said, "And it can't come true unless you eat the cookie."

Nancy smiled demurely and began to eat the broken cookie, staring into Bud's hazel eyes.

Michelle giggled like a schoolgirl. "Now who's blushing?"

***

The bedside clock read 3:15 when Bud woke suddenly. "The bandage," he said out loud, "Pierce has a bandage on the index finger of his left hand. That's what's been nagging me." He almost smiled as he pulled the blankets up around his shoulders and went back to sleep.

***

At 0730 he called Control to let the night dispatcher know he was at the station. He made a pot of coffee. He impatiently watched the clock and tried to stay busy signing time sheets, frowning at the reaction he could expect from Tom Lynch about the amount of overtime used on the Gooding case.

He put a stack of "Wanted" flyers on his desk and began going through them, committing details to memory of those faces belonging to people who might even remotely pass through his county. Sipping his coffee, he reminded himself to buy some creamer to cut the acid in the damned stuff.

Then he gimped down the central hall to Howard Finch's door. Howard was late, as usual. But as Bud turned to walk back to his own office, Howard came down the hall with his typical bustle, a full briefcase in one hand and briefs under his other arm. "Well, if it isn't the High Sheriff of Hazard. Morning, Bud."

He fumbled with the key to his door until Bud took the key and set it in the lock.

"It is a good morning, Mr. District Attorney. I bear tidings of joy and goodwill."

Howard pushed through, dumped the briefs on his desk, and dropped the briefcase in his office chair. "So, what's brings you out in the daylight?"

"I've been working the dark side. Which is to say my subconscious has been at work. I think we overlooked a wee bit of physical evidence that might link Pierce directly to the murder. If I'm right, no jury in the world will fail to convict."

"Please don't say that. Any jury can be stupid."

"They won't be."

Thirty minutes later Howard made a call to the forensic lab to take another look at the blood on Gooding's shirt. And an hour later, Bud and Howard were seated at the metal table in the interview room at the jail, with Randolph Elkins and Franklin Pierce Junior seated across from them. Elkins was in jacket and tie, and Pierce was wearing his own orange jumpsuit with "Prisoner" stenciled on the back.

"What's this about?" Elkins asked

"We'd like to know how your client cut his hand," Howard said, pointing to the Pierce's left hand.

"It's a paper cut," Pierce said a little too quickly. "Then you won't mind letting us see it," Bud said.

Elkins was genuinely puzzled. "Seems like a strange request. What's a cut on his finger have to do with this?"

"Well," Bud answered, "I think your client cut his hand on some broken glass when he reached under Gooding's shoulders to drag him to the barn and stage a fall. I think we'll find your client's blood on the deceased's shirt."

Elkins snorted. "Hell, my client isn't strong enough to move a body. Look at him."

"Then you won't mind if we see the cut," Howard interjected. Elkins looked wary, but he liked his own notion better. His scrawny client didn't have the strength to move the corpse of Gordon Gooding.

"Show them the cut, Franklin."

It wasn't a deep wound, but it wasn't a paper cut either. "Looks like you sliced it on something sharper than paper, Mr. Pierce," Bud said. "And it fits my theory. See, it's on the back of your finger, where it would be if you reached under Gooding's shoulders to grab his armpits and drag him."

Pierce glared at him.

"It doesn't prove a thing," Elkins said. "No matter how you paint it, the picture of my client moving the much larger Gooding just doesn't work. I'll kill you in court."

Bud and Howard glanced at each other and then back at Pierce.

"We'll see," Howard said, "because we are going to court. And I'd like a DNA sample from your client."

When Elkins shook his head, Howard said, "I'll get a search warrant from his house and get it that way."

"Be my guest," Elkins said.

And then it hit Bud like a revelation. It was almost as vivid as a motion picture.

"He had help. Casey was still there when you arrived, wasn't he?"

"Don't answer that."

"Casey called you on his cell phone. You both thought Gooding was dead, so you tried to make it look like an accident. You moved Gooding's body to the end of the barn. You tried to pick up all the broken glass. And then you sent Casey home and called 911. That's when you discovered Gooding was still alive, so you rolled him over and held his face in the mud until he suffocated. And then you put a muddy track on the ladder to the loft.

"You just forgot one thing. The spider webs across the open door. He couldn't have fallen through the opening without breaking the spider silk. And they were still intact."

Pierce turned pale, his hands shook, and a bead of sweat formed on his head. He reached up and adjusted his glasses, then looked at Elkins.

"You're just fishing, Sheriff," Elkins said.

"He was dead when I got there," Pierce blurted out. "I didn't kill him! Casey did!"

"Franklin!" Elkins warned him.

"Whose idea was it to make it look like an accident? Yours or Casey's?" Howard asked.

"Casey's."

"Franklin, I'm telling you not to answer the questions."

"I don't care. I want a deal."

Elkins sighed, looked at his client and then at the district attorney and the sheriff. "I'd like a few minutes to talk to my client."

When they were outside, Howard glared at Bud. "You and your damned theories. You sure about this?"

"I am, and I'm sorry, but I just couldn't get a clear picture of the crime. And then it hit me. Elkins is right. Pierce just isn't big enough to move the body by himself. As to who actually smothered Gooding, I don't know. What if they both did?"

There was silence for a few seconds. Bud looked at Howard. "Have you dropped the murder charge against Casey?"

"I was going to do that this morning."

When they were all seated once again in the interview room, Elkins said, "My client wants immunity from prosecution if he cooperates. He didn't kill Gooding, but he's willing to stipulate that he helped cover it up."

Howard tapped his chin lightly with his index finger, staring at Pierce, not looking at Elkins. Finally, he said, "You know, Franklin, you're a lying son-of-a-bitch. And I intend to prove it in court." Then he looked at Elkins. "No deal. I believe Casey's miserable story, and I don't believe your client's. I'll take my case to the jury."

Bud looked startled. Elkins was red in the face. Pierce was panic stricken, sweat coursing down his temples, face pale and hands shaking.

Elkins asked, "No deal?"

"No deal."

Elkins stood up, closed his briefcase. "Okay, then we'll see you in court."

Bud followed Howard back to Howard's office. "What the hell was that about?"

"My turn. I have a deep appreciation for your skills as an investigator. You're bright, intuitive and dogged. But this time your intuition got the best of you. I work out. Don't laugh just because I'm still a bit pudgy. Anyway, I work out at the fitness club three times a week. So does Pierce. Don't let that small build fool you. He's wiry, and he can bench press one hundred and fifty pounds. That's not enough to set records, but it demonstrates enough physical strength to drag an unconscious person seventy-five feet."

"So, you don't buy my conspiracy story?"

"No, and for the very same reason you argued when we met at your house and you blew my case against Casey. Casey was panicked; he's not the cool type. Franklin is an unfeeling, cold-blooded sociopath. He's capable of doing exactly what I'm going to make a jury believe. He tried to make it look like a cover-up, thinking we'd blame Casey, not him."

He looked up at Bud, punched him lightly on the shoulder and said, "You've done your part, Champ. Let me do mine now. Go home, or go to the cabin, get some rest."

***

Nancy was filling in her dispatch log when Bud stumped through the door to the command center. She flashed a smile and said, "Just a minute, Bud. I need to get my log caught up."

She gave him a surreptitious glance. He looked uncomfortable. Maybe it's the ankle. He should be home resting and letting it heal. When she finished the log, she looked up and said, "Well? What brings you to the dungeon?"

Turning the brim of his Stetson in his hands, staring at the floor, he stammered, "Ah…could you come outside for a minute? I'd like to talk to you."

"You can talk to me here."

The other two dispatchers were starting to grin, as though they guessed his intent.

"Well, it's personal."

"Oh. Well, in that case let's go outside. Can you guys cover for a few minutes?"

Jack Henderson, the 911 dispatcher, grinned at her, waved her out the door and said, "Got you covered."

She took his right arm and put it around her shoulders and helped him gimp down the hallway and out the front door into the early morning sun.

He sniffed the cool air, took his arm from around her shoulders and grumbled, "What's everyone grinning about?"

"Oh, I don't know. They just haven't seen a forty-year-old schoolboy asking someone for a date. At least not in quite a while." She smothered a giggle.

"I'm thirty-eight. Is that what you think I'm doing?"

She turned to stare up into his eyes. "Well, it sure better be." He stared everywhere but at her, waved at a passing car, tugged at his hat brim and finally said, "Damn, I'm just sort of out of practice. I haven't asked anyone for a date in years."

"What are you so shy about, Bud?"

"I don't know, but I was wondering if you could get a day off tomorrow. I've never had anyone out to the cabin, but I feel like I'd like to share it with someone. You know, do my show-and-tell routine, fix lunch, maybe take a ride in my boat."

She arched her eyebrows. "Someone? Linda, maybe?"

"No, no. I mean I'd like you to see it, see my photos, see my handy work, listen to the silence with me."

"Tomorrow?"

"Yes."

She stepped close and gave him a hug. "Deal. What time?"

"How about noon? I'll have something ready for lunch."

"You going out there tonight?"

"Yeah. Thought I would take Molly and head out there pretty soon."

"I'd like that a lot. Tomorrow then." She squeezed his forearms with her hands, kissed him on the cheek, and walked back to the station, hips swaying slightly, shiny black hair glistening in the sun with just a hint of auburn highlights.

He frowned, fighting an impulse to call her back and take her in his arms. He shook his head, grinned at himself, and stumped over to his pickup.

CHAPTER 13

THE FADING EVENING sun brushed the soft underside of the few puffy clouds drifting over Dog Lake. He'd wasted a lot of shots over the past several years, trying to catch the unique pastels of the desert sunset, and he had only one decent photo to show for his efforts.

Just like a gambler, he thought, focusing the cell phone camera on the dark tops of the budding willows back-dropped by a purple and rose-tinged cloud and snapping three quick shots.

He patted Molly and said, "If you painted that, the art critics would laugh you out of the business. But if you catch it on film, it's considered good photography. Wonder why that is?"

He stumped back up the short path from the dock to the A-frame, while Molly hunted the willows along the lake.

At noon the next day, or more precisely at 11:45, he heard Nancy's truck turn off the gravel and pull into the yard. Sleeves rolled up, he was at the kitchen sink washing veggies when she knocked on the door. Molly got up from her rug by the wood heating stove and barked a greeting.

Bud called out, "Come on in."

Nancy wore blue jeans, a baggy red sweatshirt with a UNLV logo, white tennis shoes, and a white baseball cap. She placed a plastic grocery bag on the counter and stooped to scratch Molly's ears.

"Hi, Molly. How you doing, old gal?" Then she straightened and looked at Bud. "There's a bottle of wine in the bag. I hope you like wine. Do you mind if I look around?"

"No, help yourself."

She walked slowly around the living area, patted the Navajo throw on the leather recliner by the wood heater, and nudged the glider-rocker to life. She climbed the ladder to peer into the loft. A neatly made bed, a nightstand, and a lamp were the only furnishings, except for two dozen wildlife photos mounted to the end wall and on the sloping ceiling.

She craned her neck to look at a large photo of a western avocet, flanked by two smaller pictures—one of a bright Northern shoveler and one of a cinnamon teal. "The birds are gorgeous, Bud," she hollered down the ladder. And then she laughed. "But why are they mounted on the ceiling?"

"Well, it's like this. I simply ran out of flat walls."

Bud had built a tall bookcase into the wall between the living area and the small bedroom and bath on the main floor. And while he was making a tossed salad, she studied the photos, looked through his books in the bookcase, and watched Bud as he moved about the small kitchen area.

She moved to the glider-rocker. "You're an interesting man, Mr. Henry Blair, and I like your cabin. So how did you become a policeman?"

He laughed. "I honestly don't know. It wasn't on my list of things to do, but I took some classes in criminology when I was in college and simply got hooked. So, I kept taking classes, and when I graduated the only place I could find work was as a cop."

"What about the philosophy books I see on your shelves?"

"Same thing. I took several classes in philosophy and got hooked there too. But I could see no way to make a living as a philosopher except to teach, and by that point I'd had enough of academia."

"Where did you grow up?"

"I grew up in the little town of Rogue River, over by Grants Pass."

"What was that like?"

"It was a good place to grow up. I had a lot of freedom as a kid, and I remember lots of family picnics and fishing the river, hiking the hills, raft trips, that kind of thing. What about you?"

"Well, I grew up in Yakima, the apple capital of the world. Daddy used his GI benefits to buy a small apple orchard when he got back from Vietnam. He also got some help from the tribe. We're Yakimas."

"I know, but where did you get those green eyes? Beautiful green eyes."

"They came from George O'Brien, my mother's father."

"Are there any other kids in your family, besides you and Sonny?"

"No. There was a younger brother, but he drowned in the irrigation canal when he was five." She paused. "We were picking apples and my cousin Alicia was supposed to be watching him. They were looking for wild asparagus along the canal bank and he fell in. Alicia was only nine and couldn't swim, so there was nothing she could do. It took her years to get over it. And I'm not sure I'll ever get over it."

"That's got to be hard."

"Yes, but life goes on."

"So, you went to Washington State University?"

"Yes, and that's where I met old what's-his-name. He taught American Indian Studies. He was tall, dark and handsome. He said he was Indian, which made it better, at least as far as my family was concerned.

"But it turned out he wasn't Indian; he was Italian. He was also a liar and he couldn't keep his hands off his google-eyed female undergraduate students. So, I divorced him.

"I went home and helped Daddy with the orchard for a couple of years. And then Daddy had a heart attack, and Sonny didn't want to be a farmer, so we sold the orchard and Mom and Daddy moved into town. He died two years ago. The doctors said it was congestive heart failure. I don't know. I think it was related to the war, but nothing can change it, so I never pushed on it much."

"So, if you introduced me to your family, would it be a problem that I'm not Indian?"

She gave him a wry smile. "No, we've gotten over that prejudice."

"Tall, dark and handsome, hmmm?"

"I suppose if we compared his photograph to yours, Bud, he would be considered more handsome by some people. But the women who know you think you're one of the most attractive men on the planet. You're a whole person. He was just…pretty."

She paused. "What would your family say about me?"

He laughed. "They would say you are beautiful. Then ask what the dickens do you see in me."

"Are you close?"

"I guess we were when Mom was still alive, but she died from lung cancer about five years ago. Dad owns a hardware store in La Pine now. And my brother Carl is a bleeding-heart liberal who doesn't like cops. He's teaching at Southern Illinois University. I think the last time I saw him was when Mom died. I miss my nieces and his wife, Maddy. And I guess except for my Uncle Ralph, Mom's brother, and a couple of cousins, that's it." He stopped, embarrassed by the personal revelations.

She just looked into his eyes and said nothing, waiting to see if there was more.

"Well," he said brusquely, "I didn't mean to talk about that. Let's crank up the barbecue and get some steaks going."

"Why don't you rest that leg. I can burn a steak with the best of them. You tell me where things are to be found, and I'll fix the lunch."

Bud sat on a kitchen chair on the narrow deck by the front door of the cabin, Molly sitting beside him while Nancy lit the barbecue and finished making the salad. He couldn't keep his eyes off her, embarrassed when she caught him staring at her. She smiled slightly and said, "Let me see your dock while the grill warms up."

"Okay." He rose from the chair and started down the short path to the dock.

"I meant I could go look. You rest your ankle."

"Yes, ma'am." He watched the slim form disappear behind the green foliage of the willows that grew along the bank behind the dock, Molly padding along behind her.

He backed up to the kitchen chair on the small deck, sat down and took a deep breath. "Damn, this feels good. Ankle and all," he said quietly to himself. It was less than five minutes before Nancy and Molly came hurrying back up the path from the dock.

"That's a nice boat. Could we go fishing after lunch?"

"You like to fish?"

She flashed him a smile. "Does a bear…? I mean, yes, I like to fish. And after lunch, I would very much like to go fishing."

"I'd be delighted to be your host and guide," he grinned back at her.

Halfway through the steak and salad, he looked across the table at Nancy and said, "How old are you?"

"That's not a question you ask a woman on the first date."

He cut another bite of steak, sipped the wine in his coffee cup and said nothing. But she could see he was digesting this bit of information.

Finally, he said, "We aren't exactly strangers, and we have had lunch a few times."

"But not a date," she said. "I consider this our first real date."

***

Bud admired Nancy's skill with the spinning rod, at least when he could direct his attention to something other than the woman herself. Despite their best efforts, the water in the lake was too cold for the bass that sulked the day away.

They switched to worms and bobbers, fishing in against a bed of water lilies, and caught a half dozen yellow perch late in the day, Molly barking each time they cranked another fish into the boat.

"That'll give us a supper mess," Bud said when the sixth or seventh fish was in the live well. "Had enough?"

Nancy nodded, patted Molly on the head and said, "For now."

"Let's head for the barn then."

At the dock, Bud filleted the fish, and Nancy said, "I see there's more to the High Sheriff than meets the eye."

"I also rank number one in the world when it comes to cooking yellow perch."

The sun had set, the fish had been eaten along with the last of the tossed salad, and the wine was gone. Bud banked the fire in the wood stove, and some soft jazz was playing on the little boom-box he kept at the cabin. Nancy sat in the glider and rocked quietly, not saying much, just soaking up the quiet and the peace of the moment. Bud was almost prone in his recliner, hands clasped behind his head, a half-smile on his lips, listening to Miles Davis and his sweet trumpet, congratulating himself for not getting asshole drunk.

"Thanks for a nice day, Bud."

"Nicest day I've had in years. We should do it again."

"I'd like that, and I hate to spoil the moment, but I have to work tomorrow, so I think I'd better head back to town."

"You okay to drive?"

"Of course. The wine is out of my system by now."

"You could stay."

"Don't you tempt me. I'm going back to town."

Bud sat up. "There's a lot of deer out this time of evening. You might hit one."

She laughed, "I think I'd better take my chances with the deer." She rose and walked to the door. Bud got out of his chair and gimped after her. She turned, gave him a quick hug and a peck on the cheek before he could react. "I like you, Henry Bud Blair.

Thank you. This is the nicest date I've ever had." She looked down at the tail wagging black Lab. "And thank you too, Molly."

Bud listened as the sound of her pickup faded down the gravel road. Then he sighed, turned off the music, sat down in the recliner and said, "Molly, this is the first time I ever felt lonesome out here."

CHAPTER 14

Monday came sunny and bright. Black-capped Oregon juncos hopped, scratched, and flitted about at the feeder in the small pine tree between the cabin and the garage. They were early feeders, and one of the few species to stay the winter. Bud often wondered if it was just because he kept the feeder full during the cold months.

The lake was glassy. A light steam lifted from the cold surface. The flat rays of the morning sun were lighting the pine trees on the ridge tops.

He watched the birds, but his mind was on Nancy. His cell phone rang, and he hoped it was her.

"Hello."

Howard Finch's deep voice said, "I need you here at ten o'clock this morning."

"Well good morning to you too, Howard. What's up?"

"Just be in my office at ten hundred."

"I'm trying to take a few days off!"

"I need you."

"Okay, okay. I'll be there, but you're spoiling a perfectly nice day."

"Good. You deserve it."

"Why you unsympathetic…" but the line was dead. Bud stared at the cell phone, turned the power off, and set the phone on the counter.

Molly stood by the back door and looked expectantly at Bud. "You hungry?" He let her out and poured some dry food into her dish by the back door. "We've got to go to town. Good thing I'm only sort of laid up. I don't know what would happen if I was really in bad shape. Probably get me off my deathbed. At least we'll see Nancy when we're there. Maybe go to lunch. And you can't go."

It was 8:30 when Bud dropped Molly in the back yard of the house. He drove to the station and parked in his Reserved-Sheriff parking spot.

Michelle looked up and smiled when he pushed open the front door. "Morning, Sheriff. How's the ankle?"

"The ankle…let me see." He looked down at the walking cast. "Yep, still attached."

"Okay, I'll stop asking."

He smiled back. "Actually, the ankle's doing okay. But my hip and my right arm are sore as hell."

"I thought you were taking some time off."

"I did, one whole weekend, but Howard called this morning and told me—note I didn't say asked me—to be in his office at ten. Wouldn't say more than that. Just 'Be here.'"

He pointed at the pile of books and articles on her desk. "Are you studying?"

"Amy Woodruff gave me some articles and some books to read about spousal abuse. I'd like to understand how the victims got that way. It's like they feel that, somehow, they failed their husbands and they are to be blamed, so the punishment is deserved. Some men are victims, too. The ones that are the hardest to understand are the unmarried women who stay with their live-in boyfriends.

"I can't really see a pattern, although some of the victims were physically abused as children. The psychology of those seems to run along the lines of something like, if that's the only attention you got as a child, it's normal, and it's better than no attention at all. That's almost understandable.

"But the ones I can't understand are those who were raised in decent homes by apparently caring parents. There seems to be a common thread of low self-esteem, passive behavior, that kind of thing. But some women…they are mostly women…stay in abusive relationships sometimes until they are killed, in spite of repeated beatings.

"And I didn't know it was so common. But when you include the cases of psychological and verbal abuse, it looks like an epidemic."

She paused, took a deep breath. "And the abusers are hard to understand. In the case of live-in boyfriends, the real risk is to the children, especially babies and toddlers. About the only thing I can compare it to is the tendency of tomcats to kill the mama cat's litter. Just get rid of them. I talked to a caseworker at Services for Children and Families. She said there were several infants killed last year in our fair state when judges refused to take abused children into protective custody."

She banged the desk with her fist. "That's just bullshit. Damn their eyes! They should be reading this stuff, not just me."

"So, do you understand the victims?"

"No. Even after I read all this material," she said, pointing to the stacks of book and articles, "I still can't understand them."

"I don't either." He gimped over to the coffeepot, the walking cast making clunking noises. "By the way, you heard anything about Melissa Casey? How she's doing, that kind of thing?"

"As a matter of fact, Amy Woodruff called to let me know Melissa and Lucinda are moving back to the ranch. Apparently, she feels safe now that her husband is in jail. And Judge Hopkins denied his bail. Said he was a flight risk and a risk to the community."

"Well, that's good. It'll keep her daughter in the same school with her friends."

He sat down in the swivel chair, propped the cast on a plastic visitor's chair, sipped his coffee, and said, "Thanks for making the coffee…again."

"A small courtesy from an underling."

"Not going to let it go, are you? Where's Sonny?"

"Oh, I almost forgot. He's gone to Burns to interview two cowboys our friends in Harney County arrested yesterday afternoon. And the Callahan's brought us a piece of the wire they think was used to repair the fence where the rustlers cut it. Sonny said he's going to see if he can get some samples of wire at the Johannsen Ranch. We might get a spectrographic match. No two rolls of wire are the same, I'm told."

"The experts say that," Bud agreed. "Well, maybe we'll get that case wrapped up, too."

He picked up the phone and dialed Roger's number. Tom Johnson answered. "Outpost number one. How may I help you?"

"Morning, Tom. I take it Roger isn't in?"

"No, he said he was going to take another run to Christmas Valley and do some vestigating."

"Vestigating?"

"Yeah, that's what he called it. Vestigating."

"And I suppose you'll tell me the difference between vestigating and investigating."

"Well, he said 'investigating' was based on some insight, some intuition, some inside knowledge, and since he didn't have any insight, intuition, or inside knowledge about his meth informant, only some sad suspicions, he would have to settle for 'vestigating.'"

Bud laughed. "Okay, thanks. How're you doing these days?"

"Oh, you know. It's the same old same old. Talk about budget cuts and moving all the Forest Service law enforcement officers here in the deep southeast to Bend or Klamath Falls. It doesn't make sense, but then it doesn't have to."

"Well, good luck. We'd hate to lose you."

"I'd hate to go."

"Talk to you later."

Michelle's eyebrows were raised in question when Bud hung up. "Hate to lose you? You don't mean Roger?"

"No, no. That was Tom on the phone. He said there were rumors about moving the Forest Service law enforcement officers to Bend or Klamath Falls."

"That's dumb."

"Yep. I think I'll call the forest supervisor and find out what's going on. I need Tom where he is."

She looked at Bud. "Well, at least we'll have another deputy for Roger to partner with."

"You know, Deputy Trivoli, I'm wondering if we shouldn't quietly hire a new deputy and have him work undercover in the north county area. Roger thinks something has happened to his informant. Actually, he hasn't said so, but what he thinks is that someone offed the guy. So maybe if we have an officer working undercover, we might get a line on that meth lab. That might lead us to the whereabouts of the missing informant."

"It should be a woman."

"What?"

"A woman. Have a woman work the bar at the Christmas Valley Lodge. Druggies have big mouths."

"Whatever happened to male supremacy?"

Michelle grinned. "You'll still be the boss, Bud, for now."

"You think I'll be working for you one of these days?"

"Maybe."

"You after my job?"

She grinned. "No, I think I'll just run for the county judge's seat." She turned serious. "Bud, we did miss my six-month review. And you gave me a long, hard look after I spouted off about intending to shoot that Casey son-of-bitch. Do you doubt my ability to do this job?"

"Hmm. We have been kind of busy these past few days. Okay, informally, because we'll have to do a formal one later, I think you're a good law enforcement officer. You exercise good judgment in critical situations, you interview well, you're a keen observer, and no, I don't have any doubts about your ability. It's just that your intensity about William Casey surprised me. That's all."

"You sure? Because if you doubt me, I'll look for another job."

"Oh Michelle, if I could only get down on bended knee, I'd beg you to stay."

Her eyes turned misty, and she blinked to keep the tears back. "I want to stay, and I want you to trust me."

He rose from his chair, leaned over the desk and held out his right hand. "Shake on it."

She gave him her soft, warm hand and formally and firmly squeezed. "Deal."

He took his hand back, grinned and said, "What's up with you and Charlie?"

She frowned. "Charlie's a nice guy, but I think he's too ambitious for me. Lives for his job. He called last night and said he was going on some special assignment on the coast before coming back here."

"Well, he's young and bright and has a good future in the state police."

"Well, I pity the woman who hitches her wagon to his star then. Ambition has its place, but too much is…what?…ugly, bad manners, unseemly…I don't know."

"How about calling it a grievous wound."

The phone interrupted. Michelle picked it up. "Sheriff's Office, Deputy Trivoli." She listened intently, making notes. When the caller had finished, she said, "Okay, Mrs. Johnson, give me your address. I'll be there in about thirty minutes. No, that's fine. I'm glad you called."

She hung up. "A Mrs. Guy Johnson. Says some boys have been drag racing past her place out in the West Side area. She says they almost ran her down when she was checking her mailbox. So, she took her camcorder and got them on tape the next time they went by. She says the license numbers are clear, and she has identified one of the boys. Ain't modern technology great?"

Bud shook his head. "Yep. Not like the good ol' days. So, what are going to do with these dragracers?"

"Depends on how mad Mrs. Johnson is."

He watched her pull away in the county's white Ford Explorer, the sun glinting off the side windows as she turned the corner.

Nancy answered on the first ring. "Control. Nancy Sixkiller."

"Good morning, Nancy. I guess you didn't hit any deer on the way home."

He could hear the smile in her voice. "No, I managed to avoid the denizens of the woods, but I must have seen thirty or forty of the critters, and I had to come to a complete stop to keep from hitting a mommy and a Bambi."

He laughed. "I'm glad to know you're safe. How about having lunch with me?"

"Well, she said suspiciously, she could do that, but does he have some ulterior motive?"

"Yes," he answered, "and he's hungry too."

"Are you in town, or are you inviting me back to the cabin?"

"I'm in town. Been summoned by our worthy DA for some mysterious meeting at ten. So, I thought we could have lunch."

"Like in 'date'?"

"Like in two good friends having lunch."

"Like in…date-lunch," she amended.

"Sounds like it. Meet me at Plush West at noon?"

"I'll be there."

A staggering pile of files, flyers, memos and advertisers begged for attention, spilling onto the desk. He sorted the papers by month, started in on the March pile, sighed and then pushed it aside. "Later," he muttered, and picked up the last two copies of the Lake County News that someone, probably Karen, had placed on the corner of his desk. He snorted. Even Asa couldn't help but wax poetic.

The banner headline read: "Daring Dawn Raid".

"Early Saturday morning, a team of law enforcement officers from the Lake County Sheriff's Office, the Oregon State Police, the Lakeview Police Department, and the U.S. Forest Service, surrounded a hunter's cabin on the slopes of Drakes Peak northeast of Lakeview, Oregon.

"Led by Lake County Sheriff, Henry (Bud) Blair, the posse captured William Casey, a local rancher wanted for criminal assault and for murder in connection with the death of Gordon Gooding, a longtime Lake County resident and rancher.

"Sheriff Blair was injured when the suspect discharged a rifle, killing the horse the sheriff was riding. The horse fell and rolled on the sheriff's leg, breaking his right ankle. The Lake County Ambulance Service transported Sheriff Blair to the Lake County Hospital for treatment."

The article described Officer Trivoli returning the gunfire, protecting the injured Sheriff while the other officers closed with the suspect and subdued him after a brief struggle.

Bud couldn't find anything specific to fault with the coverage. He just didn't like to see his injuries discussed in the papers. And to call his team a posse was romantic bull. He thought about walking to the newspaper office to talk to Asa but discarded that as too hard on his ankle. He picked up his phone.

Asa answered on the first ring. "Lake County News."

"Asa? Did you write this thing?"

"Do you mean the article praising the good work of our local law enforcement?"

"That's the one," Bud growled.

"Didn't you like it?"

"I liked the part about my officers, but 'A daring dawn raid'?"

"You'll note it is bylined. That was Carol's story. I'm not going to edit this rag forever. And I think she was proud of her special friend, Officer Sixkiller, for capturing Casey."

"I missed that."

"Apology accepted. How's the ankle?"

"Damned fine."

"Did you watch the K-Falls news? The TV coverage of Pierce's arrest?"

"Missed it."

"Well, they edited out your 'No comment' scene. It was good, objective news coverage. I hoped you had seen it. They could've made you look like a hick-town cop if they had chosen to do so.

I taped it, so if you want to see it sometime in the future, let me know. Anything new to share with your faithful scribe?"

"Well, Harney County arrested two men in connection with the cattle rustling that's been going on out in the Warner Valley. Sonny Sixkiller is off to the metropolis of Burns to question the suspects. And, I had a summons from our esteemed DA to meet him in his office this morning. But he wouldn't tell me what that's about."

"Hmmm. The mysterious DA, huh?"

"The irritating DA is more like it. Well, just wanted to say thanks for the story."

"Come by and have a cup of coffee one of these days."

"I will. Thanks."

He hung up. Asa thinking of retirement? It was hard to imagine. He sighed again and turned back to the stacks of mail. "I thought the undersheriff was supposed to take care of this stuff." At ten o'clock he clunked down the inner hallway of the courthouse to Howard Finch's office. The door was open. Howard was on the phone, but he nodded and waved Bud in.

He heard Howard say, "Thank you for the information. Will you testify to those facts when we go to trial? Thank you, Mr. North."

Howard slammed the phone down—he always slammed the phone down regardless of his state of mind—and said, "Bud, all hell's breaking loose. And I love it." He laughed and snorted, his mop of blond curls bouncing "You know what they say about rats leaving a sinking ship?

"That was John North. He said there was an anonymous letter on his desk this morning detailing a scheme by our friendly banker Franklin Pierce to embezzle funds from his own bank. North said he made a cursory audit this morning, and it looked like it was true. He's calling in the Feds to conduct a thorough audit."

"Good lord!" Bud said. "Murder and now embezzlement. If you looked at that little rat, you'd never suspect a thing. He looks respectable and harmless all at the same time."

"Yes, but there's more. At 10:30, you and I are going to receive two visitors. That's why I wanted you here. A certain Ms. Susan McDowell and her attorney, a woman from Bend, are to share some information with us related to murder and embezzlement."

"She wants a deal?"

"Nothing was said about a deal, but I'll eat my daughter's dirty diaper if they don't ask for one."

"Do you know this attorney?"

Howard looked at his notepad. "Her name is Martha G. Pitney. I don't know her. Do you?"

"No. I'm sure I've never even heard of her."

"Okay. And just to keep you in the loop, Elkins has decided that he can't represent either Casey or Pierce without violating client confidentiality. It would be a conflict of interest. So they'll each have to find a new attorney."

"I guess it would. If he claims Pierce only helped move a body, he convicts Casey, and makes Pierce an accessory after the fact. And if he claims Pierce actually killed Gooding to defend Casey, he convicts Casey of assault. I think I'd run for the hills myself." And then he laughed. "Damn it, Howard. This thing has more threads than a spider web."

"Ah, my friend, I don't think we've found them all yet. Wait and see. There's one more strand being spun as we speak. Oh, what tangled webs we weave..." Howard intoned.

"And speaking of spiders," Bud began, "I did some reading. You know how we thought the spider webs proved Gooding couldn't have fallen out of the loft? Well, according to the National Audubon book on insects and spiders, an orb weaver, think barn spider, can weave a new web overnight."

Howard looked only mildly interested. "Oh well, I wasn't planning to use that in court anyway."

At precisely 10:30 a trim woman in a gray skirt and jacket knocked on the open door and smiled. "Mr. Finch? I'm Martha

Pitney. I've asked my client to wait until we've had a chance to speak. Is that all right?"

"Please come in, Ms. Pitney."

Howard rose and walked around his desk, hand outstretched. Even with two-inch heels on his cowboy boots, she was an inch taller than Howard. Say about five feet nine. Wearing a wedding band. An ink stain on the middle finger of her right hand. A fountain pen, maybe a holdover from her college days? Like Asa and his pipes? Age, about fifty, fifty-five. Nice figure. Probably works out. Pleasant face, but steady eyes and firm mouth. A disciplined, dedicated attorney. Rested and fresh looking. The only incongruous item: a western bolo tie. A horsewoman or an affectation?

"Thanks for coming, Ms. Pitney. This is Sheriff Henry Blair," Howard said.

Bud rose from his chair and shook hands. "Good morning."

She frowned and said, "Good morning, Sheriff. I hope you're not planning to arrest my client."

"No, no, nothing like that," Howard said a little too quickly. "I asked the sheriff to sit with us because he is the chief investigator on the Gooding case. He can help me check the facts, should there be any, of your client's story."

"Well, first I'd like to talk to the Lake County District Attorney, alone," she said. "And then we can decide."

She's already taking charge, Bud thought.

Howard looked at Bud. "I'll be in my office," Bud growled.

Forty-five minutes later, Howard called. "Come on back. I need you now."

Susan McDowell was seated beside Martha Pitney to the left of Howard's desk. A vacant chair was on the other side.

"Sorry, Sheriff, but I needed to get some ground rules straight," Martha Pitney said.

Bud sat and said, "That's all right." His tone said it wasn't.

Howard cleared his throat. "Well, let's get started. I'd like to tape record Ms. McDowell's statement."

Martha nodded and Howard started the tape recorder. "This is Lake County District Attorney, Howard W. Finch. With me is Lake County Sheriff, Henry Blair, Martha Pitney, attorney for Susan McDowell, and Susan McDowell. The date is April 24, 2000. Time is 11:45 a.m. Ms. McDowell has been sworn. Ms. McDowell, is the statement you are about to give me of your own free will?"

In a soft but firm voice Susan McDowell said, "It is."

"All right. In your own words, then."

She cleared her throat and without looking up began, a slight tremor in her voice. "I have been having an affair with Franklin Pierce. It wasn't my choice, but he pressured me, hinting that if I didn't cooperate, I'd lose my job. I'm alone in the world, no family living and no close friends, so I was afraid that if I didn't give in, he'd fire me."

"How long has this been going on?" Howard asked.

"A little over two years, but I took a good performance rating that John North gave me—he's my boss—and sneaked off to Newport and applied for a job in a bank over there. I start work in three weeks."

"Why didn't you apply earlier?" Howard asked.

She looked up, a hint of tears in her blue eyes. "Because I didn't have anything to use against Mr. Pierce. All he had to do was call the bank and I wouldn't have gotten the job. But when I discovered he was embezzling from his own bank, he didn't dare interfere any longer. That's when I asked Mr. North for an evaluation and a reference."

"And North will corroborate this?"

"Oh, yes sir. He most definitely will. He told me he was sorry to lose me."

"You weren't involved in helping Pierce with his embezzling scheme?"

"No sir." She stared at the floor, and then looked directly into Howard's eyes. "But at first I was afraid it would look bad for me, too. I'm sure that several of the girls at work had a suspicion that

Mr. Pierce and I were having an affair. If only they knew what he put me through!"

Howard stared at her for a minute, and then asked, "Why did you come forward at this time?"

"I have a degree in accounting. So I went looking. I could find nothing in the records that could implicate me. That's when I confronted him, told him he was a thief, and that I was leaving. And that's when he told me he had killed Mr. Gooding. He started saying all kinds of nonsense about having done it for 'us,' that the Gooding ranch was going to be a destination resort. That we'd be rich, and he could leave his wife and quit the bank. That kind of thing. Why, I was shocked. I didn't love him. I can't imagine what made him think I wanted anything to do with him."

Bud had been watching without saying anything. Finally, he cleared his throat. "Can you be more specific about what he said about killing Gordon Gooding?"

"Well, he said he had control of the Gooding ranch. I asked him how. He said he'd loaned Gooding some money, so he had a lien against the ranch. I said something like, 'You mean the bank?' And he laughed and said he'd personally loaned Gooding the money, not the bank. So, that meant he was going to wind up owning it. He tried to make Gooding's death look like an accident, but he said he wasn't worried, because if the police found out Gooding had been killed, they'd blame Bill Casey."

"Okay," Bud said, "Now how did he embezzle the money, and how much did he take?"

"I don't know how much he took, and I only found one case. It was a simple deal. He endorsed a loan to a Van Duzer, processed it through the bank at about two percent less than he charged Van Duzer, and then pocketed the difference. It really didn't amount to much."

She nodded to her attorney. Martha Pitney opened her battered briefcase and produced a file. "You'll find the evidence you need in here."

Howard spoke into the microphone. "Let the record show that Susan McDowell is giving me a file that allegedly supports her claim that Franklin Pierce Junior was embezzling from his own bank."

"Oh, it will, Mr. Finch. It will."

"Are you willing to testify in open court that Mr. Franklin Pierce told you he killed Gooding? And that you copied documents proving he embezzled from the bank?"

"Yes, to both questions, Mr. Finch."

Howard spoke into the microphone again. "End of interview." And he switched off the tape recorder. "I'll have this typed and ready for your signature by three this afternoon. I'll expect you back at that time. Okay?"

Martha Pitney answered, "We'll be here, Mr. Finch. You keep your part of the bargain." And then she and Susan McDowell rose and walked out the door without another word.

Bud looked at Howard. "Well?"

"Well, what?"

"So, what's the deal?"

"I gave her immunity from prosecution. No charges as an accessory after the fact, although she was a wee late in coming in. And we get her testimony. That should cook Pierce's goose."

"And you believed her story about being coerced into an affair, and her ignorance of the embezzlement?"

"Sure. Why not?"

"Because she is lying through her teeth. It's too pat. The story is too neat, and her memory too clear. Either she rehearsed her story, or her attorney coached her. I'd bet money she's behind the embezzlement, that she framed Pierce and played him for a dumb schmuck. And I'll bet when the feds audit the books, they'll find Pierce was embezzling a lot more than a few bucks skimmed off one account. And Pierce won't have a dime to show for it."

"Oh, you do have a suspicious mind, Bud."

"No, just too many interviews with too many liars. This one was a marvelous liar, and a damned good actress. Did you notice the tears?"

"Yes. Most convincing."

"Then you don't fully believe her either." It wasn't a question.

"Not entirely, no. But I do believe Pierce was embezzling, with or without her help. And he did kill Gooding. As for her part, we'll never prove it one way or the other, unless the feds turn something up."

"What about your deal?"

Howard grinned, a big wolf grin, lips skinned back from his teeth. "Oh, if they find she's broken a federal law, that will be a different matter. It won't be Lake County that charges and prosecutes then."

"You're a devious bastard, Howard."

"Yes, I know. It's one of my better qualities." Bud laughed. "So it is, Howard. So it is."

CHAPTER 15

June had come and gone before a trial was set for either William Casey or Franklin Pierce Junior. Bud gave a deposition to the attorney for William Casey, a Klamath Falls attorney named Boston Smithers. He also he gave a deposition to an Eldon J. Priest, an attorney from Medford who represented Franklin Pierce Junior. Howard supervised both depositions and wondered aloud why they bothered since he was going to put Bud on the witness stand anyway.

***

Rocked back in a reclining lawn chair on his dock, soaking up the early afternoon sun, he watched Molly hunt the willows again for maybe the third time that day. A totally bare hook hung below a bobber. "Fishing for dumb ones," he laughed at himself.

He worked Saturday shifts again because Saturday nights were a busy time for the police force. And he'd started taking the county's pickup to the cabin on Sundays so he could respond to calls without going all the way back into town to pick up a rig. His ankle healed, but it was a little tender yet, and his fellow sheriffs still called and ragged him, wanting to know if he'd killed any horses lately. But in his mind, the Casey and Gooding cases were behind him.

Harney County was insisting they prosecute the rustling suspects for other rustling ventures and for vehicle theft. Howard was debating about trying them a second time for rustling regardless of the outcome of the Harney County trial.

"I do have my hands full right here though," he muttered to Bud. "Those cowboys rolled on each other and on a greedy butcher in Nyssa, so I don't imagine they'll beat it in court. Well, we'll see."

Earlier in the week, his officers told him they wanted to hire a woman named Larae Holcomb for the undercover assignment in Christmas Valley. Her employment file reflected the career of an intelligent, dedicated officer. But when they showed him a picture, he winced.

In the photo, Officer Holcomb was sitting on a big Harley, wearing a tank top and pointing to a tattoo of a snake on her left shoulder. And she had what could only be described as a shit-eating grin on her face.

"She's perfect," Roger said.

"You're serious?" Bud asked.

"Very much so."

"She looks rough as a cob."

"That's the general idea," Sonny said.

Bud shook his head and then said, "Okay, do it. When does she start?"

Roger turned serious, none of the good ol' boy in his manner. "I have a job lined up for her as a barmaid at the Christmas Valley Lodge. She'll start next month. I have communications worked out, and I'm moving up there a month after she gets in place. She's not to do or say anything for the first thirty days. Just listen and build her cover."

Bud looked at Sonny. "You're the undersheriff. What do you think?"

"It'll work, and Roger has all the bases covered."

Michelle clapped her hands. "I like the way things work around here."

Bud's cell phone rang. He sighed and pulled it from the pocket of his fishing jacket. "Damn the cell phone company and their new towers," he muttered. "I used to have a little peace and quiet out here."

But his mood lifted when he heard Nancy say, "Hello."

"Hi, Nancy. You coming out?"

"No Bud, not today. But…" She paused. "Well, I have a week's vacation coming. The Colonel said he would cover for me. I was wondering if you could get some time off?"

"Whoa! My heart's about to jump out of my chest. Where would you like to go?"

"Oh, I don't know. How about the coast? We could walk the beach, now that you're healed up. Eat fresh crab. That kind of thing."

"I think I could do that."

"Good!"

"Pick you up at six in the morning?"

"No."

"What do you mean, 'No?'"

"I'm only about three miles from the lake. I lied about coming out."

"Oh, hell. I don't have much to eat, and I'm fishing with a bare hook."

She giggled. "That's okay. I'm bringing steaks, and if I can't stay tonight, I'm throwing them out."

"I do love steak." He punched the cell phone off, and then he laughed, a good wholesome freeing laugh.

He reeled the bobber in, stuck the hook in the handle of the pole and hollered at the little black Lab. "Molly, you rascal. We're having company."

***

He leaned the fishing pole up beside the door and stumped upstairs, Molly ran tail-wagging behind him, feeding on his excitement. He pulled the throw rug back, pushed down on a floorboard and slid it forward revealing a hidden compartment with a small fireproof safe. He spun the dial, cussed and started the sequence over again, "Take your time, Bud."

This time the combination worked and he swung the lid back. He took a deep breath, reached in and took a tiny, velvet-covered jeweler's box from the safe.

For a minute, he just held it, and then he opened the box and showed Molly a shining, sparkling diamond ring.

He bent down and scratched the dog's ears. "Molly, I love that woman so much I'm afraid I'll mess things up. But I'm going to ask her to marry me, and I hope and pray she says yes."

He turned and started down the stairway as he heard Nancy's pickup turn into his driveway.

EPILOGUE

SUSAN SIGHED CONTENTEDLY, put the computer disk back in the false bottom of her desk drawer, and called to her puppy, a half-grown German shepherd. "Come on, Buck. The tide's out. Let's go for a walk on the beach."

Even with over $479,000 scattered in various money markets, savings bonds, treasury bonds, and savings accounts, some in her dead grandmother's name, the only modest extravagance she allowed herself was the cash purchase of the condo overlooking South Beach and the dunes across Yaquina Bay from Newport, Oregon.

She liked the area, and she liked her new job as a teller in the America's Bank. She told herself she was through with the game. She was out and she was staying out.

***

Duane Witherspoon, Treasury agent and computer sleuth, went over the accounts again. He called Special Agent Warren Simpson, agent in charge of the FBI's Seattle office.

"Hey Warren. This is Duane. How you doin'?"

"Duane, old buddy. You never call unless you need some help."

"Not true. You keep forgetting the tickets I got us to the Seahawks game."

"Hell, Duane. That was over three years ago."

"That long? Well, you know, life happens. You remember that banker in Tacoma who embezzled about a quarter of a million dollars from his own bank?"

"Vaguely."

"Well, he keeps making noise from that country club prison he's in. Claims all he was doing was testing the bank's computer security system."

"To the tune of a $250,000?"

"Yeah, I know. Anyway, he keeps saying his girlfriend actually took all the money."

"So?"

"This is where it gets interesting. There's a similar case in southeast Oregon. Someplace called Lakeview."

Sounding a bit more alert, Special Agent Simpson asked, "What's the kicker?"

"It seems this small-time banker embezzled over $200,000 from his own bank."

"And?"

"So, now we have a second banker singing the same song. Says his girlfriend, who just happens to have the same name mentioned by our guy here in Seattle, engineered the whole thing."

"Coincidence?"

"Do pigs fly?"

"So, what do you want?"

"Well, all embezzlers keep a ledger. That's part of the game, sort of a score card. We get the ledger, and we get the thief. Understand?"

"And you think we have enough evidence to take to a federal judge and get a search warrant."

"Yeah. I do. Let me bring my files over and show you. We get a warrant, we tear her place apart, we find the ledger, and we send her away."

"What about a safe deposit box?"

"No. In my experience, these guys and gals keep it close by, like some kind of security blanket."

"Or like a mean dog that bites the owner. Okay. Bring your files on over, and we'll take it from there."

"Warren. I want a piece of the action."

"Okay. You got it."

ROD COLLINS has done a little of everything: teacher, newspaper editor, logger, truck driver, soda jerk, construction worker, wildland firefighter, fire lookout, aerial observer, and business consultant.

More important, he is a devoted husband, father, and grandfather.

And, like Louis L'Amour, he has walked the land his characters walk.

Spider Silk is the first of the Sheriff Bud Blair Mystery series followed by *Stone Fly, Bloodstone, Mariah's Song,* and *Not Before Midnight.*

Rod's post-Civil War adventure novels feature Captain John Bitter in *Bitter's Run* and *Abiqua.* In non-fiction, *What Do I Do When I Get There?: A New Manager's Guidebook* is Rod's award-winning business reference guide.

Visit brightworkspress.com to learn more about his work. You can also chat with Rod on his personal blog: brightworkspress.com/blog.

www.ingramcontent.com/pod-product-compliance
Lightning Source LLC
LaVergne TN
LVHW041711070526
838199LV00045B/1292